"There's son

Leah smiled, bu
before."

John studied her expression. "What do you mean?"

"Nothing. I didn't mean anything. It's just an expression."

John wasn't sure he believed that, but he didn't want to push her. He had already done that too much this conversation. He gave her a little smile. "Well, if you've heard it before, then it must be true. There *is* something about you."

Leah inhaled. Their eyes stayed locked on one another's. He stepped closer to her. His mind shouted at him to stay back, to keep his distance emotionally and physically.

She had said that she did not want to get married to anyone, ever. He was finished with casual dating. And yet, he could not force himself to back away. His heart pounded as he gazed down at her. The rising moon cast a silver glow across her features.

She looked beautiful in a plain, honest way. He wanted to hold her hand...and tell her that he was falling for her.

After **Virginia Wise**'s oldest son left for college and her youngest son began high school, she finally had time to pursue her dream of writing novels. Virginia dusted off the keyboard she once used as a magazine editor and journalist to create a world that combines her love of romance, family and Plain living. Virginia loves to wander Lancaster County's Amish country to find inspiration for her next novel. While home in Northern Virginia, she enjoys painting, embroidery, taking long walks in the woods and spending time with family, friends and her husband of almost twenty-five years.

Books by Virginia Wise

Love Inspired

An Amish Christmas Inheritance
The Secret Amish Admirer
Healed by the Amish Nanny
A Home for His Amish Children
The Amish Baby Scandal

Sisters of Stoneybrook Farm

His Amish Christmas Surprise

Visit the Author Profile page at LoveInspired.com.

HIS AMISH CHRISTMAS SURPRISE

VIRGINIA WISE

Recycling programs for this product may not exist in your area.

ISBN-13: 978-1-335-62113-9

His Amish Christmas Surprise

For questions and comments about the quality of this book, please contact us at CustomerService@Harlequin.com.

Love Inspired
22 Adelaide St. West, 41st Floor
Toronto, Ontario M5H 4E3, Canada
www.LoveInspired.com

Printed in Lithuania

And I will give them an heart to know me,
that I am the Lord: and they shall be my people,
and I will be their God: for they shall return unto me
with their whole heart.

—*Jeremiah* 24:7

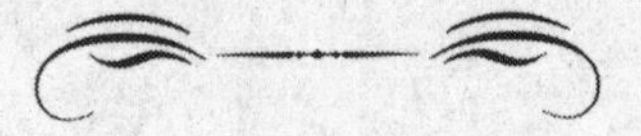

To Abigail

Chapter One

Leah Stoltzfus stood at the kitchen counter of her family's farmhouse rolling out gingerbread dough when she heard a cry in the distance. She set down the rolling pin and listened. At first, she thought it must be one of the animals. She and her four siblings raised goats, and they had a habit of slipping out of their pen at night, especially when her twenty-one-year-old twin brother, Benjamin, accidently left the gate open.

Leah heard another high-pitched wail, carried by the wind. That did not sound like a goat. Leah frowned and stared out of the kitchen window, but all she could see was her own reflection in the dark pane of glass. She spun around and marched out of the kitchen, brushing her flour-coated hands on her apron as she went. Her footsteps echoed against the high ceilings of the old house as she hurried down the entry hall.

"Hello?" she called out as she threw open the front door.

There was no one there.

Their Anatolian shepherd, Ollie, stood a short distance away, ears alert, whining softly. The guard goose, Belinda, honked and hissed from inside the goat pen, across the farmyard.

Then Leah heard the cry again, this time clearly. Her

attention shot downward, to the noise. Leah gasped. There was a newborn baby at her feet, wrapped in a fuzzy pink blanket, tucked into a car seat.

She dropped to her knees and reached for the baby. “Where have you *kumme* from?” she asked as she pulled the baby from the carrier and into her arms. The baby stopped crying and nestled closer. “You poor, sweet thing,” Leah cooed as she snuggled the child.

Leah desperately wanted a child of her own. But she refused to open her heart to any man who could potentially share that future with her. She had made that mistake once, and she would never make it again. Steve McCrary was a charming *Englischer* she had met during her *Rumspringa* a year ago. He had swept her off her feet in a whirlwind romance. They used to talk for hours about how they would make the future work. Maybe he would convert. Or maybe she would jump the fence to be with him out in the *Englisch* world. Either way, they would be together. Forever. Because she trusted him, she let things go too far between them.

Then Leah learned that he was engaged to another woman—while still declaring his love to Leah. Steve and his wife were married now, with a baby, and living in Philadelphia. Last Leah had heard, they were very happy together. She had learned two things from the humiliation and heartbreak. One, never trust an *Englisch* man to keep his word. Second, never fall in love again. Ever.

Single motherhood wasn’t the Amish way, but Leah had held out hope that *Gott* would find a way. Now, her prayers had been answered. The love and loneliness stored inside of her poured out into this tiny, vulnerable person who needed her.

Leah glanced over at the family's guard dog. "You were keeping watch, ain't so?"

Ollie's tail flicked slowly from side to side as he stared at the baby with dark, expressive eyes.

"You understand that we need to protect her." Leah inhaled the sweet scent of baby as she pressed her face against soft, blond curls and kissed the top of the child's head. "I'll keep you safe." It was not an idle promise. She meant the words. This baby was her responsibility now. After all, hadn't *Gott* led this baby to her doorstep? And hadn't He watched over the situation so far? It was an unusually mild evening for December, so the baby had stayed warm and safe until Leah found her.

"Leah?" Benjamin's voice rang out from the farmyard before his boots thudded up the front porch steps. "What have you got there?"

Ollie whined, then loped up the steps to stand beside Benjamin.

Leah glanced up at her twin brother and smiled. "A *boppli*."

"*Ya*, I can see that. I meant *why* do you have a *boppli*?"

"Because *Gott* sent her to us."

Benjamin took off his black felt hat and scratched his head, leaving his dark brown hair sticking up. He shoved his hat back on his head and glanced around. "But where is the *mamm*?"

"I don't know."

"Oh, boy."

"Actually, I think it's probably a girl. See the pink blanket?"

Benjamin rolled his eyes, but he was smiling. "*Ya*, I see. You know what I meant." He absentmindedly reached down to pet Ollie's head.

Leah returned the smile, then carefully stood up while clutching the baby to her chest. "We need to get everyone together for a family meeting."

"And the bishop too."

"*Ya*. Can you run over and fetch him?" Bishop Amos and his wife, Edna, lived across the split rail fence and down the hill, on the neighboring farm. Benjamin was married to Amos's niece Emma, so the families were especially close.

"Sure." Benjamin stepped closer to get a good look at the baby's face.

"She's cute. I just wonder who the *mamm* and *daed* are. She doesn't look like anyone we know."

"*Nee*. She's *Englisch* for certain sure. Amish parents wouldn't buy their baby a car seat."

Benjamin nodded. "You know, I've heard of *Englischers* abandoning a *boppli* with an Amish family. They think we provide *gut* homes."

"That's because we do," Leah said with a smile. She ran a finger over the baby's warm, soft skin.

Benjamin frowned. "Don't get any ideas now, Leah. This *boppli* doesn't belong to us."

"I'm not getting any ideas, Benji." Leah was already planning their future together, but she would not admit that, of course. Not yet anyway. "Regardless, I intend to do everything I can for her. She's my responsibility now." Leah did not tell Benjamin that this baby was an answer to her secret prayers. It was too humiliating to explain the entire story. Her siblings suspected that she had fallen for an *Englischer*, but they didn't realize how serious Leah had been about the relationship. And they did not know that he had discarded her for another woman after Leah had gone too far with him.

Benjamin looked at Leah for a moment, then shook his head and trotted back down the steps. Ollie followed close behind. Benjamin stopped and turned around. "You don't know much about *kinner.*"

"I babysit your *boppli*, don't I?"

"That's not the same," Benjamin quipped.

"I know it isn't."

"Just making sure you do."

Leah waved Benjamin away. "Just go get the bishop, okay?" She knew her brother was right, but she was not going to admit that. She was too desperate to fill the hole in her heart to accept logic. Leah shifted the baby in her arms as she watched her brother and their dog hurry across the farmyard and disappear into the night.

"We better get Miriam," Leah murmured to the baby. "She likes to think that she's the boss around here." After their parents passed away in an automobile accident with a hired *Englisch* driver a decade ago, Miriam had taken on the job of raising the four younger siblings. Leah giggled and touched the tip of the baby's nose with her finger. The baby made a gurgling noise that Leah interpreted as a laugh. "But we will do what we want to, ain't so?" Leah knew that her sisters must be in the production building, where they stored and pasteurized the goat milk, or in the goat shed, making sure the herd was tucked in for the night. Her sister-in-law, Emma, was putting her baby, Caleb, to bed upstairs. His name was actually Benjamin, after his stepfather, but this was too confusing. In the Amish naming tradition, he would be called Benjamin's Benjamin to clarify. But this was confusing and cumbersome too. So, they used Benjamin's late father's name, Caleb. Pretty soon, everyone had shortened Caleb's Benjamin to Caleb.

Leah was getting ahead of herself, thinking about naming traditions and what she could call the baby to make her one of the family. "Let's take a walk to the barn," Leah said as she sifted through Amish girls' names in her mind. She could not help it. "You can meet the goats while I look for everyone."

But before Leah made it off the porch, yellow headlights swept across the front yard, followed by the crunch of gravel beneath tires. Leah squinted against the bright light and stepped forward. She couldn't see past the glare of the lights. "Who's there?" she asked loudly.

The engine turned off, dropping the farmyard into silence. Leah could hear the baby's soft breath in the quiet. The wind whispered through the bare branches of the oak tree and a goat bleated in the distance. Leah tightened her grip on the baby as a fierce wave of protectiveness surged through her. The light from the headlights disappeared, allowing Leah to make out a red two-door sedan with a dent across the hood. She stared into the darkness, trying to make out the details. The door swung open with a creak, and two legs wearing heavy black work boots slid out, landing on the gravel with a thud.

Leah stared as a man emerged from the car. He was tall and good-looking, with chiseled features, brown hair and a muscular build beneath his red flannel shirt and worn jeans. "Hey!" the man called out as he stormed across the gravel driveway. "That's my baby!" He did not take the time to close the car door, leaving the interior light shining into the farmyard and a soft chime repeating into the silence.

Leah took a quick step back.

The man stumbled to a stop. "Sorry, didn't mean to startle you. But I've got to get my child."

"Now, just wait a minute." Leah drew herself up to her

full height of five feet three inches and raised her chin. "I don't know who you are, but I do know you can't just take back the child that you abandoned."

"I didn't abandon her." He took a step closer.

Leah took another step back.

The man sighed. His eyes were on the baby. "Look, I don't want to cause any trouble. I just want to make sure my baby is okay."

"She's fine."

The man nodded. "I'm just going to come up on the porch and make sure, all right?"

Leah frowned. "I don't know who you are. Why should I trust you? If you care so much, then why did you leave her here?"

The man shifted his weight from one foot to the other. His eyes never left the baby in Leah's arms. "I told you. I didn't leave her. Her mother did."

Leah swallowed hard. She was not used to strange men showing up on her doorstep, claiming abandoned babies. He seemed sincere, but how could she be sure? Steve had seemed sincere too. "You've got a lot of explaining to do."

"Okay. But will you please let me come up on the porch?" A flicker of vulnerability passed over the man's stony features. "I just want to hold my baby girl."

Leah stared back at the man. Beneath his hardened expression and large-framed, muscular build, he looked lost, panicked even. There was more to this man than his outward appearance. Leah felt a rush of sympathy for him, but she could not let her emotions get in the way. The baby in her arms came first. She would not let this man a step closer until she knew for certain sure that his intentions were good.

And that would take an awful lot of explaining.

* * *

John Mast stared at his baby girl. His heart felt so full and so empty at the same time that it left his mind reeling. His arms ached to hold the child, but he forced himself to stand still. The woman on the porch looked nervous, and he didn't want to scare her. He tried to see the situation through her eyes—a baby appears on her doorstep, followed by a strange *Englischer* rushing toward her. He swallowed hard. "Is she healthy?"

"I think so."

John exhaled. "How long has she been here?" He tried to make out his baby's face, but the pink blanket blocked his view.

"I just found her a few minutes ago. Now, tell me who you are and why your baby is here."

John moved his attention from his baby to the woman who held her. She looked to be around his age and had light brown hair tucked beneath a white *kapp*, a fair complexion and a light spray of freckles across her nose. She was not smiling. "I didn't know I had a baby until tonight," he said.

The woman's eyes narrowed.

"I just got a text from Haley, her mother. I hadn't heard from her since..." John rubbed the back of his neck. He wanted to be respectful. "...well, since the one night we were together. It was a mistake. For both of us." His gaze moved back down to his baby. "But she's not a mistake."

The woman nodded.

"I didn't know that I was a father. But now that I do, I intend to do right by her."

"I don't understand. Why didn't the mother leave the baby with you?"

John looked away. He remembered the brief time he

had spent with Haley. He could see how she would have made assumptions about him. She must have seen him as the kind of guy who was out to have a good time without taking any responsibility. She did not know that the night they spent together was the only time he had allowed loneliness and fear to tempt him down the wrong path.

"You don't have an explanation?"

John sighed. "Haley left a voicemail saying that she left the hospital a few days ago and couldn't handle having a newborn baby. She wants her to go to a good stable home, which she didn't think I could provide. But she still wanted to give our baby a chance to know her dad, especially since she won't know her mother." His jaw flexed. "She doesn't know me very well. I am not abandoning my child. I can give her a stable home. I am not just going to just visit her occasionally. I'm going to raise her."

The woman's face was unreadable. "Have you tried to talk to Haley since then?"

"Yes. She blocked me after leaving the voicemail."

"*Vell*, did the voicemail explain why she chose us? We're strangers."

"She always thought the Amish were good people."

"We are. But still..."

"Yeah. I didn't know Haley very well, but I know that she wished she could have been born Amish. She said it was too late for her now, that there was no way she could convert at her age. Not after she grew up with internet and electricity and everything. She said that she couldn't give it up." John's memory sharpened as he replayed that conversation. "She said that if she ever had a baby, she would want it to be raised Amish and have a better chance at life than she did. Her childhood was difficult. Foster homes, no real family, no community. She thought the

Amish had all of that. Haley had a pretty wild life and must have known she couldn't take care of a child. By leaving her baby with you, she believed she was doing the best thing for her."

"But why my family, specifically? There are lots of Amish families around here." The woman leaned forward, her expression anxious, as if she hoped for a certain answer. John didn't know what she wanted to hear. He hoped she would accept the truth.

"Haley's voicemail didn't go into any detail. Just that she had stopped by an Amish farm to buy goat milk soap for the baby and found a family who would give our child a good home. She said they seemed full of love. I guess you must be part of that family."

"I guess so, but I've never seen this *boppli* before. I didn't meet the *mamm*."

"She said she just sat in the car and watched you all for a while, then drove away."

"It's not a coincidence," the woman murmured. "Of all the farms..." Her eyes looked thoughtful and faraway.

"Hello, there!" a man's voice called out behind him. John spun around to see an elderly Amish couple, followed by a young Amish man who looked a lot like the woman on the porch, but with darker features. The big brindle-colored dog trotting alongside him growled when he saw John. "Easy now," the young man said quietly.

"I'm Amos Yoder, the bishop for this church district," the older man said as he hurried forward. He was small and elderly, with a sharp nose, rosy cheeks and a wizened expression. "And this is my wife, Edna." He motioned to the woman beside him. She was taller than Amos and had a plump figure, making her husband look even smaller in comparison.

"You *oll recht*, Leah?" the young man asked loudly. "Who's this *Englischer*?" He was talking to Leah, but looking at John.

"My name is John. I'm this baby's father."

Amos stared at John. "John?" He furrowed his brow. "I think I recognize you. John Mast, right?"

Heat spread through John's body. He tugged at the collar of his shirt. "Yes. That's me."

"The John Mast from Little Creek, down in the next church district?"

The young man crossed his arms and kept staring at John, but said nothing.

John sighed. Of all the places for his baby to end up, why did it have to be with the Amish? Was that why Haley had been attracted to him in the first place? An *Englischer* with an Amish background—the best of both worlds in Haley's troubled mind? Would he never get away from the past? "Yes. That's me."

"I knew it." Amos chuckled and shook his head. "You sure have grown. I'm surprised I recognized you." John wasn't overweight, but he was big, broad shouldered and tall. He was used to people commenting on his size. But he was not used to those comments coming from anyone who knew him from childhood, before the eighth-grade growth spurt that made him a head taller than his peers. "I'd like to see my baby," John said quietly. He had had enough with the small talk.

Amos hesitated. His smile faded. "You've been gone a long time, John."

"I know."

"Have you come home to stay?" Amos asked.

John felt the muscles in his shoulders tighten. He forced himself to relax. "This isn't my home anymore."

"This will always be your home."

"Will someone please tell me what's going on?" the young woman asked. Her eyes narrowed as she stared at John from the porch. "Are you Amish?"

"No." John sighed. "Not for a long, long time, anyway."

She looked surprised for an instant, but the expression was quickly replaced with the no-nonsense look she had been wearing since they met. She glanced at Amos and he nodded. *"Oll recht,"* she said to John. "You can hold her." But her expression was not enthusiastic.

John rushed up the porch steps and gently eased the baby from the woman's arms. Their eyes met briefly, and he could make out the green flecks in her brown irises. Her skin felt warm and soft as she shifted the baby to him. And then the world faded away as John held his baby for the first time. He could not believe this tiny, perfect being was his own flesh and blood. He stared down at her, trying to see himself in her face. She had his mouth, for sure. A big, goofy grin spread across John's face. He could not stop smiling. And then his daughter opened her eyes and stared directly at him. Nothing had prepared him for that moment of connection. He thought his heart might burst.

"Why don't you come on inside, John?" Edna said.

John's attention shot back to the people around him. "I, uh, should just take my daughter and go. No need to go to any trouble on my account."

"No trouble," Edna said.

"Edna's right," Amos said. "We should talk."

John frowned. He was going to have to accept the invitation, no matter how uncomfortable it made him. The truth was, he needed whatever support he could get in order to give his baby a stable home. Twenty minutes ago, he had been completely on his own, trying to find his place in the world. Now, he was a father with a life-long responsibility. "Okay," he said. "Let's talk."

Edna motioned toward the young man and woman. "This is Leah and Benjamin. This farm belongs to them and their sisters."

Leah's and Benjamin's expressions stayed guarded. "I'll go get everyone," Benjamin said, then shot John a look before he walked away toward a weathered, unpainted barn.

A wave of nostalgia swept over John as he stepped inside the rambling farmhouse. The old building reminded him of his childhood home. So did the flickering propane lamp that lit the spacious living room, casting shadows across the bare, cream-colored walls and sparse furnishings. The only wall decor was a simple advent calendar with a manger scene printed on it. A blue rag rug lay on the scratched hardwood floor, and a handmade quilt covered the back of a worn couch. A row of wooden chairs and a glider with embroidered cushions faced the couch. A black woodstove sat in the corner beside a stack of wood, and a magazine rack stuffed with old copies of *The Budget* newspaper. The window sills were decorated with fresh greenery and white candles. The tiny flames flickered against the dark glass, making the room feel like an old-fashioned Christmas.

"Take the glider," Leah said. "For the *boppli*."

"Thanks," John said as he sat down and shifted the baby's weight in his arms. Her little body relaxed as he began to rock. Amos and Edna settled onto the couch.

Leah hovered near John, watching the baby. "*Vell*, I better get some *kaffi* and cookies," she said after a moment. But she did not look eager to leave the baby's side.

Amos leaned forward as soon as Leah left the room.

"Where have you been? How are your parents? We've worried about you."

"And prayed for you," Edna added quickly.

"Ya," Amos said.

John exhaled. Where to begin? He was glad when the sound of the front door interrupted them, followed by multiple footsteps. Benjamin shot into the room, followed by three women who looked to range in age from their early twenties to early thirties.

"This is Miriam," Edna said. "The oldest Stoltzfus sister." Miriam was short and compact, but her fierce expression made up for her small size. She clutched a piece of paper in her hand. "Amanda," Edna nodded toward another small woman with dark features and tanned skin. "And Naomi." Naomi was taller and thinner than her sisters, but her dark hair and eyes marked them as siblings.

Leah hurried into the room carrying a tin decorated with snowmen. "I didn't take the time to pour the *kaffi*. I hope no one minds if we just have cookies for right now. What did I miss?"

Benjamin chuckled. "Nothing yet."

"Gut," Leah said, then handed the cookie tin to the bishop. "Pass it around."

The bishop popped open the lid and smiled. "Molasses crinkles. My favorite." He grabbed three big cookies, and John wondered how Amos stayed so thin with such a big appetite. The man had not gained a pound since the last time John saw him, a decade ago.

Leah turned her attention to John as Amos handed the tin to Edna. "How do we know this *boppli* is even yours?" Leah asked.

John flinched. She was not going to make this easy.

Miriam lifted her hand and waved the paper in the air. "It's all here."

"What have you got there?" Amos asked.

"The *boppli*'s birth certificate. I searched the car seat before we came inside."

"It says the father is John Mast." She strode across the room and handed the document to the bishop. He shifted all his cookies into his left hand and took the paper with his right one. He studied the words for a moment, then gave a quick nod. "Sure does."

"*Ya*, but how can we be sure this is really John Mast?" Leah asked. She made a sharp motion toward John, while keeping her eyes on Amos. "What if he's an imposter?"

Benjamin laughed.

"It's not funny, Benji," Leah snapped.

"I remember him, Leah," Amos said.

"We both do," Edna said.

"It's easy to prove," John said. "I'm *Englisch*." He couldn't help but admire Leah's attitude, even if it was a bit irritating. She cared about the baby's welfare, that was clear. John tightened his grip on his daughter, leaned forward in his seat and pulled his wallet out of his back jeans pocket. "I've got my driver's license right here. That's all the proof you need."

"I'll take a look," Leah said. She marched across the room with her chin held high and plucked the ID from John's hand. Amos and Edna exchanged a glance but said nothing. Leah frowned as she studied the driver's license.

"Not my best photo," John said.

Leah did not smile at his attempted joke. She just moved her eyes back and forth from the photo, to John, and back to the photo again. Then she made a noise in the back of her throat and handed the ID back. "Fine. It's you."

Amos and Edna chuckled, then quickly cut off their laughter. Amos cleared his throat. "John, can you fill us in on what's happened to you since your parents moved your family away from Little Creek?"

John leaned back into the glider. His hand began to move in slow circles over his daughter's back. "Not much to tell, really," he said after a long silence.

"I'm sure there's something to tell," Miriam said as she made her way to the row of wooden chairs and sat down. Amanda and Naomi followed close behind, but Leah kept hovering near John's shoulder. "Leah, sit down," Miriam added. "You're making us all nervous. You too, Benji."

Benjamin shrugged and glanced at Leah. She rolled her eyes before they both dropped onto the big couch beside Amos and Edna. Leah did not lean back against the cushions. Instead, she stayed perched on the edge of her seat, tapping her foot as she waited.

"I guess you know that my parents didn't just leave Little Creek, they left the Amish as well," John said.

"Ya," Amos said.

"They didn't adjust so well. Got to drinking, staying out when they should have been home. Had some trouble with the law, here and there." John sighed. "You know how it is. My sister had her troubles as well. It hasn't been easy."

"And what about you, John?" Amos asked.

"*Ach*, I don't know." John frowned. Had he just slipped back into Pennsylvania Dutch that easily? He would have to be more careful. "I've done okay, I guess." He had not always been okay, but this was not the time to talk about that. He had been lonely for years, caught between two worlds, belonging nowhere. His parents were too busy with their own problems and temptations, leaving him to figure things out for himself as he forged a path among strangers.

"Where are they now?" Edna asked.

"California, last I heard."

"You don't keep up with them?" Amos asked.

"No. It's better this way. I'm not Amish anymore, but that doesn't mean I agree with the way my parents live."

"And your sister?"

"I've lost touch."

Amos slowly shook his head. "I'm sorry to hear that, John."

John force a quick smile. "It's fine. Not a big deal."

Everyone in the room looked as if they disagreed. The silence was painful. The only noise was the creak of the glider and the distant bleat of a goat somewhere beyond the living room walls.

"Vell." Amos slapped his hand on his thigh. "Let's figure out what we're going to do about this *boppli*."

John knew what he needed to do—stand up, grab his daughter's birth certificate and walk out of the farmhouse forever. He needed to put his daughter in the car and drive far away, where he could escape every childhood memory and every reminder that he was supposed to be Amish. Why had he even come back to Lancaster County in the first place? And why did he feel this tug to a past that he had spent a decade running from? That was the question that he had been asking himself ever since he returned a year ago.

And he still could not answer it.

Chapter Two

Leah wanted to jump up, march over to John and pull the baby from his arms. She resisted the urge, now that she knew the baby was his. But how could she know if he would be a good father? Was her responsibility to this child really over?

Her heart said it was not. Not when she had prayed for this moment for so long.

The room felt tense with silence. Amanda shuffled her feet, and Naomi adjusted the skirt of her dress. Amos chewed a bite of his molasses crinkle cookie as he studied the birth certificate in his hand. "Says here the baby's name is Abigail." He tapped the paper, then looked up at John. "It's a *gut* name." Amos gave a meaningful look. "A *gut Englisch* name *and* a *gut* Amish name."

John looked away when he caught the implication in Amos's words. "She's not Amish," he said quietly.

"She could be," Amos said.

John didn't answer. Instead, he took the child's tiny hand in his. His fingers looked enormous next to hers. "She's too little for such a grown-up sounding name. We'll call her Abby. *I'll* call her Abby," he quickly corrected himself.

Amos and Edna looked at one another. Edna nodded

at her husband. "*Vell*, John, you and Abby will be needing some help, ain't so?"

"No. We'll be fine."

"You've taken care of a baby before?"

John frowned. "This is the first time I've ever held one."

"You've got *Englischers* to help you?" Miriam asked.

"Uh, well..." John shifted in his seat. "I don't really know anyone outside of work. I work a lot. Haven't really had time to meet anyone."

"What do you do?" Edna asked.

"Construction. I'm on a crew building houses on the other side of the county. I've got a studio apartment over there. It's not much, but it'll do."

"Who's going to watch Abby while you work?" Leah asked. She leaned forward. "You can't leave her alone, you know."

"Of course I know that!" John clamped his mouth shut and shook his head. "Sorry, didn't mean for that to come out like that. I just meant that I know enough about babies to understand that they need a lot of care. I'm her father. I'll figure it out."

"*Ya*, I'm sure you will," Amos said. "If a new mother can figure these things out, a new father certain sure can too." He raised a forefinger. "But, that doesn't solve the problem of childcare. Someone's got to watch this *boppli* while you work construction all day."

"I'll find a day care."

"Day care is very expensive, John," Edna said. "Do you make enough money for that? And, even if you do, it won't be easy to find one that will take such a young baby on such short notice."

"Uh..." John cleared his throat. "I don't have any extra money. I live paycheck to paycheck."

Leah threw up her arms. "Then who's going to take care of this *boppli*?"

"I don't know." John lifted one of his hands from where it rested on the baby's back and rubbed his forehead. "I'll find a way."

Leah knew what she wanted to do. This baby was her responsibility. She had known that from the moment she had first seen her, innocent and helpless, on her own front porch. She did not stop to think how rash or naive this might be. "I'll watch Abby during the day. She'll be safe here."

Everyone's eyes swung to Leah.

All of them but John knew that the declaration made no sense. Leah had made it clear that she was not interested in getting married. She told everyone that it was because she wanted to focus on other things, like the business classes she was taking—with Bishop Amos's permission, of course—so she could help manage the farm better. And she claimed that she wanted to experience life a little. Maybe even travel. The *Ordnung* didn't allow her to fly, but she could take a bus to Pinecraft, Florida. Or maybe to one of the Amish settlements out West.

Those reasons weren't lies exactly. There was some truth in them. But mostly they were a way to cover up the deeper truth. Leah was too ashamed to admit what had happened with Steve and how much he had hurt her. She could not tell anyone that she had sworn off love because of him. No one knew that she secretly prayed for a family of her own—without the man attached. They would not understand or approve of that. Her siblings saw her as the carefree sister, the one who just didn't want to settle down yet. She let them believe that.

"*You*, take care of a *boppli*?" Miriam asked.

"You can never get Caleb to stop crying," Benjamin said.

Leah pursed her lips. Benjamin was right about that. She had never been able to get him to settle down when he had colic. But who could? Babies cried. That's just what they did.

"And you said you needed more time to study for those exams you've got coming up," Naomi said. "You've been saying you've got to get that business certificate to help Miriam out."

Leah didn't respond. She had built up so many excuses for staying single that she couldn't explain now. Especially in front of the bishop and an *Englisch* stranger.

"Babysitting would take up your study time," Amanda said.

"I don't need your charity," John said. His eyes met Leah's, and she felt a brief spark flare between them. Was it pride on his part? A need to prove himself? Or something else? Whatever the feeling, it left her unsettled.

"Now, wait a minute," Amos said gently. "Leah's got a point."

"Leah doesn't know any more about babies than John does," Miriam said.

"I help out with Caleb!" Leah said, a little louder than she had intended.

"She tries," Benjamin said and chuckled.

"Benji, you can wipe that smug look off your face, thank you very much," Leah said.

Benjamin grinned as he raised his hands in surrender.

"What's going on in here?" a voice said from the living room doorway. Everyone's attention swung to where Benjamin's wife, Emma, stood with her hands on her hips. "It's past nine o'clock at night and I can hear you all clear as day upstairs, in Caleb's room. What are you all doing up? It'll be time for the morning milking before we know it." Her gaze cut to Amos and she frowned. "Is everything *oll recht*? Is there some kind of emergency?" Then her eyes landed on John. "And who are you?"

Benjamin laughed and patted the empty chair beside him. "Everything's *oll recht. Kumme* sit. We have some catching up to do."

"I'll say," Emma said, then laughed.

A few minutes later, Emma shook her head. "*Vell*, I sure missed a lot putting our baby to bed. Tomorrow night it's your turn, Benji."

A round of laughter passed through the room.

Leah was ready to get back on subject. She needed this problem solved, and she didn't like that no one seemed to trust her to take care of a baby. "They don't think I can take care of Abby." Although, to be fair, it was her own fault. She had pushed that narrative to keep them from setting her up with eligible men who wanted to start a family with her.

"Oh." Emma's eyes shifted to her husband. "You said that?"

"*Ach*, not exactly."

Emma raised her eyebrows.

"Oll recht," Benjamin said. "It was pretty close to that, I guess."

Emma shook her head, and Benjamin shrugged, then smiled sheepishly.

"Leah's perfectly capable," Emma said. "And I think we should all support her." Emma hesitated. She looked down. "I remember how scared I was to be a single *mamm* of an *Englischer's boppli.* Who knows what might have happened if Benji hadn't asked me to marry him?" She swallowed hard and her cheeks reddened. "Benji took on a baby that wasn't his…"

Benjamin moved his hand to cover Emma's. "That baby is mine now, just as much as if he had always been mine."

Emma smiled and squeezed Benjamin's hand, but she did not raise her eyes. "The least we can do is help to give this baby the care and attention that she needs. As Amish, we help others, especially when we've been in a similar situation, ain't so? It's the right thing to do."

"Thanks," John said. "But I'm not Amish. I'm not one of you."

"You were Amish," Amos said quickly. "You could be again."

John shook his head. "It isn't that simple."

"Few things worth doing are simple," Amos said.

"Look, I really appreciate you all offering to help me. But I can't make any promises or commitments. I'm *Englisch* now."

"Then why did you return to Lancaster County?" Edna asked. "Little Creek is a long way from California."

John sighed and looked away. "I can't make any promises to any of you."

"We're not asking you to," Amos said. He shrugged and his eyes twinkled. "Just pointing out some facts. Maybe those facts will grow on you."

"Maybe," John said. He gave Amos an even stare. "And maybe not."

Amos shrugged again, but that twinkle did not leave his eyes.

"I'll help Leah," Emma said. "We've already got all the

supplies we need, since Caleb is only a few months older. We can all pitch in when need be."

"Ya," Benjamin said. "I'll help."

"Me too," Amanda and Naomi said at the same time.

"I'm just over the fence," Edna said. "I can *kumme* over anytime to help."

"It takes a village," Amanda said.

Everyone but Miriam chimed in to agree. She was studying John carefully. "You'd have to follow our rules when you're here. And you'd have to let us treat Abby as Amish. We will be speaking Pennsylvania Dutch to her, and we won't be acting fancy, that's for certain sure."

"I haven't accepted your help yet."

"You don't have a choice," Leah said. She felt a fierce need for him to agree. She would not let him take Abby away, never to be seen again.

John was silent for a moment before he nodded. "All right. I accept. And, uh, thank you. I appreciate it. Not sure I feel right about it though. I'll pay you what I can, but it won't be what you deserve."

"We're not doing this for money," Leah said.

John nodded again. "I understand. Thank you. Even so, I'll pay what I can." He adjusted his hold on Abby and stood up. "I better get her home and let you all get to bed."

"Wait," Emma said. "You need supplies. I've got extra diapers."

"You'll need formula and bottles too," Benjamin added.

"*Gut* thing her *mamm* left her here in a car seat," Miriam said.

Fifteen minutes later, the Stoltzfus and Yoder families were standing on the porch, watching John's car wind down the long, gravel driveway. The yellow headlights cut through the darkness as they swept across the silent, sleeping landscape of green fields and pastures.

"*Vell*, that was unexpected," Amanda murmured.

They all laughed, except for Amos, whose eyes stayed on the car until it disappeared from sight behind a cluster of oak trees. He was usually the first to laugh at any joke, so Leah wondered what he was thinking.

"Maybe not," Amos said. "Maybe *Gott* has a plan at work here. I never stopped praying that the Mast family would *kumme* home again."

"John didn't seem very eager to rejoin the faith," Miriam said.

"Nee," Amos said. "I'm afraid he's going to fight it every step of the way. But deep down, he knows who he is. He knows where he belongs."

Leah stared into the blackness at the end of the driveway. In the starlight, she could just make out the silhouette of trees and the curve of the hill that led to the peach orchard and the pond at the edge of the Yoder property. She remembered Abby's sweet baby smell and how right it had felt to hold her. She was relieved that John had seen reason. That baby belonged here, with the Amish, whether or not John wanted to admit it. Leah felt a surge of excitement at the thought of helping the child, of making a difference. But there was more to it than that. This might be her only chance to raise a baby, unless she was willing to let a man back into her heart. She knew she could not do that. She had an iron will. That was a quality the Stoltzfus sisters were known for, whether for good or for bad.

The problem was that this baby did come with a man attached. Sort of. They didn't have to have a relationship. They didn't even have to be friends. But it was still going to be complicated. She did not trust John, despite his supposed good intentions. Good intentions did not always equal good actions or good results. Would they be able to get along and keep this unexpected arrangement?

Leah was not sure. But she would do everything she could to make it work.

John was exhausted when he pulled into Stoneybrook Farm the next morning. As soon as he dropped Abby off, he would have to double back the way he came, to his worksite an hour's drive away. His pulse throbbed in his ears and his body ached from lack of sleep. And, Abby was wailing in the back seat as if the world were coming to an end. He could not put the car in Park and turn off the engine fast enough. He jumped out, popped the seat forward and maneuvered his large frame around the seat to unbuckle his daughter. Two-door cars were *not* designed for car seats. He had chosen the beat-up sedan from the used car lot because it had been cheap. Of course, he had not anticipated he would ever need to use the back seat. And certainly not for a baby.

"There you are," a woman said from behind him.

John recognized that voice. He sighed as he slowly pulled Abby from her car seat and contorted himself to ease them both out of the car. "Hey, Leah."

She stood with her arms crossed, frowning at him. "Running late, ain't so?"

"There was an unexpected incident involving an extra diaper change, then there was spit-up..." He shook his head. "Never mind. We're here now."

"*Gut*. No need to stay. We'll take it from here." She held her hands out.

John passed Abby to Leah. Even though he was desperate for a break, his arms felt empty as soon as he let go of her. "I'd like to make sure she's okay. You know, see that she's adjusted to strangers before I leave."

"You're a stranger to her as much as we are," Leah said.

John flinched. She was right. "Still…"

"Suit yourself. If you want to be late for work, that's on you."

The farmhouse's screen door swung open and Amanda appeared in the threshold. "Invite him in for breakfast," she said loudly enough for her voice to carry to the driveway. "Where are your manners, Leah?"

Leah looked back at Amanda. "He's late for work."

Amanda moved her hands to her hips. "Aren't you usually the friendly sister?"

"Not when it comes to situations like this."

Amanda ducked back into the farmhouse, and the screen door banged shut.

John was staring at Leah when she turned back around. "If you have a problem with me, it's best we clear the air now. I want this to be amicable. I know you're doing me a favor, but I don't appreciate feeling like I've done something wrong." He didn't like confrontation. He would rather let it go, but he couldn't pretend that everything was okay. "If you don't like me, just say so and we can try to avoid one another."

Leah sucked in her breath.

John kept staring at her. He couldn't help but notice how cute she looked as she peered up at him with her brow furrowed. His jaw tightened. He would not entertain any thoughts of Leah being cute. This was a necessary arrangement for the good of his daughter. Not a friendship. And certainly nothing *more* than a friendship.

"*Vell*, you don't have to look at me like that," Leah said.

"Like what?"

"Like you're so irritated with me."

Thankfully, she had read his expression as irritation. It would start them down a bad path if Leah suspected that he had been thinking how cute she looked when she was annoyed. He shouldn't have been thinking it in the first place.

"Pretty sure you were the one irritated with me," he quipped back.

Leah grunted.

"So, what's your problem with me, anyway?" John sighed. "I didn't mean that to sound combative. I'm seriously asking. Because we need to get along, right? For Abby's sake."

"*Ya*. We do." Leah paused long enough to kiss the top of the baby's head. "I don't have anything against you. I just don't trust you. I don't know anything about you. The bishop vouches for you, but it's been a long time since he knew you. You were just a child then."

John felt the familiar shame creep up his spine. This was why he avoided the Amish. They never trusted him. As soon as they heard he had once been one of them, they made all kinds of assumptions. He had never been baptized, so he had not been shunned when his family left. He had not had any choice about leaving when he was twelve years old. Yet, he still felt the consequences every day.

The *Englisch* weren't any better about accepting him. As soon as they heard the Pennsylvania Dutch accent, they peppered him with questions. When they learned his background, they considered him a novelty, a fun story to tell their friends. They did not see him as one of them. And he didn't feel like one of them either. John could never get used to the distance between them. The conveniences that the *Englisch* enjoyed—cell phones, streaming platforms, flat-screen televisions—separated them from one another. They didn't take the time to connect with each other, not when they had a screen to occupy them instead. Even the modern, everyday luxuries like air conditioning pulled neighbors apart. When John was growing up Amish, the adults used to sit on their front porches on summer evenings after the work was done, while the children ran through the neighborhood, waiting for the house to cool down enough to go inside to bed. People talked during those long, humid evenings. They laughed together and shared their lives.

He had heard the *Englisch* talk about being lonely, but then they would shrug their shoulders, as if it were just a fact of life. Those were the times when John felt an aching need for his childhood community, where he had never known loneliness. Neighbors always dropped by, women came round with pies, and the whole church district turned out for barn raisings.

But no one in Lancaster County wanted to share a life with John anymore. No one wanted to include him—they only wanted to include his daughter. He was thankful for that, but it made him even more aware that he was an outsider among his own people.

And he was an outsider among the *Englisch*. He did not want his daughter to live between worlds as he did, fitting into neither. But which world was best for her?

"You don't have anything to say?"

"Right." John cleared his throat. He had let his mind wander. The last thing he wanted to do was explain himself to this woman who could not possibly understand where he was coming from. But she was sacrificing her time and energy to help him, so he had better step up and say something. "I can't make you trust me."

Leah waited.

John stared back at her. He could hear the soft rasp of her breath and see the spray of freckles across her nose. The sunlight brought out the green hiding within her brown eyes.

"Wait. That's all you're going to say?"

"There isn't much else to say." John had learned long ago that it didn't do any good to try to explain himself. Better to hold back and say as little as possible. He could get by easier that way. Let people assume what they wanted. He couldn't stop them, no matter how hard he tried to tell them who he was.

"*Vell*, fine." Her expression did not look like she thought it was fine.

"You know, I could say the same thing to you."

Leah's eyes narrowed. "What do you mean?"

"You're a stranger. How can I trust you?"

"But I'm…" Leah didn't finish the sentence. She shook her head. "It isn't the same."

"It is to me. I'm leaving my baby with someone I don't know."

"Everyone around here knows me. They know I'm one of the Stoltzfus sisters. They know we own Stoneybrook Farm. They all come here to buy our goat milk. They trust me."

John gave a slow, exaggerated shrug and put his hands in the air, as if he couldn't understand what she meant. "Doesn't change the fact that *I* don't know you." He knew he was goading her a little, but he couldn't stop himself. Despite the hurt he felt at her judgment, he found their back-and-forth a little amusing. Leah Stoltzfus wasn't boring. He'd give her that. "The way I see it, I ought to be more concerned about you than you are about me.

After all, you're the one watching *my* baby. Not the other way around."

Leah's face reddened. She opened her mouth, then closed it again without speaking. Her lips formed a tight line as she shook her head, turned on her heels and marched across the farmyard, up the porch steps and into the house. The screen door banged behind her so loudly that it woke up the large dog dozing in the shade of the porch. The animal sniffed the air, whined, rolled over and closed his eyes again.

"So, no breakfast then?" John yelled after Leah. He could not stop a smile from appearing on his face. He did not want to feel satisfied that he had gotten under her skin, but he did. After all, he had only told the truth. He felt a little twinge of guilt, since she was volunteering to help him. But he managed to shove that feeling away. He had not asked her to help and he certainly had not asked her to criticize him. Better to get to work and forget all about their conversation as soon as possible.

So why was he still thinking about her long after he drove away from the farmyard?

Chapter Three

It had been a very long day. Leah had barely sat down since John dropped off the baby. Every five minutes she was either fixing a new bottle of formula, changing a diaper or rocking Abby to sleep—usually unsuccessfully. Now it was almost time for dinner and the thought of cooking a big meal felt about as doable as climbing Mount Everest. For now, all she wanted was a tall glass of cold milk while she put her feet up.

Abby fussed and squirmed in Leah's arms as she stood in the kitchen, wondering how to tackle dinner. Emma had run over to the Yoder farm next door to borrow some nutmeg for a pumpkin pie. Leah's sisters were all in the production building or doing the milking in the goat shed. They would be in soon, but she wanted to show them that she had everything under control when they arrived. She would prove that she knew what she was doing, since they were so smug about her lack of babysitting success in the past.

But first, she needed a cold drink. Leah cradled Abby in the crook of her arm and pulled a glass bottle of fresh goat milk out of the propane-powered refrigerator with her free hand.

"Got your hands full?" Benjamin asked as he strode into the kitchen.

"Finished with the milking?" Leah asked in return.

"Ya."

"Gut," Leah said. "Grab a glass for me, why don't you?"

As soon as Leah finished her sentence, a baby's cries drifted through the ceiling and into the kitchen. Benjamin pointed upward, to the room on the floor above them that held his son's crib. "Right on cue."

Leah laughed. "Fine, go take care of your own *boppli*. Just remember I've got it harder than you because I've got to get supper on too."

"You're a hero, Leah." Benjamin flashed a sly smile. "Maybe John will notice." Benjamin glanced at the clock on the wall. "He should be here soon, ain't so?"

"Why should I care if John notices?"

Benjamin shot her a look. "I'm your twin. I know things. There's no use pretending."

"Benjamin Stoltzfus, I am not pretending."

"Uh-huh. Then why are you giving him such a hard time?"

"I am not giving him a hard time." Leah set the milk bottle onto the counter with a sharp clang and stared down Benjamin.

"Then why did you keep grilling him with questions last night? When I wanted to court Emma, you supported us, even though she was expecting an *Englischer*'s *boppli.* You welcomed her into the family and didn't judge her, even when our sisters did."

"You were giving John a hard time too," Leah said. "I saw the way you were staring him down last night."

"*Vell*, it's not very often that strangers show up at our

house with a story like his. I wasn't taking any chances with my family."

"But now you're okay with him?" Leah asked.

"I'm still keeping an eye on him. But you're getting off subject. The point is that he's getting under your skin, not mine."

Leah narrowed her eyes. "I have not let him get under my skin."

"Then answer my question. Why give him a harder time than you gave Emma?"

"That's different," Leah said. "We had known Emma our whole lives. She's one of us."

"John was one of us too." Benjamin's expression turned serious.

"Not one of *us*," Leah said. "We didn't know his family. They're from the Little Creek church district."

"Amos and Edna knew them."

Leah shook her head. She didn't have a good argument. Benjamin didn't need to know that John brought back memories of Steve. They were both *Englisch* men after all, and both were full of promises. Sure, John's promises were about being a good father, while Steve's had been about spending his life with her. But still. Leah had learned her lesson and would not trust any sweet-talking man again—especially an *Englischer*. "Shouldn't you go get your *boppli*?"

Benjamin grinned. "*Ya*. We'll finish this conversation later."

"Don't count on it."

Benjamin began to walk away but turned back before he reached the doorway. "Leah, I know what it's like to feel different. Even if we don't trust him yet, we should still try to see things from his perspective."

Benjamin had been born with dyspraxia, also known as developmental coordination disorder, so he had always struggled to fit in with his peers. He had never been able to keep up with them in sports, and he tended to fall behind in his work.

"Benji, I didn't mean..." Leah sighed. "This isn't the same thing. We have to be sure he's a *gut* man. We can't trust him."

"I can't argue that. But you probably shouldn't drive him away while you figure it out. What happens if you decide you like him?"

"That's not going to happen."

"I think it has. Just a little bit." Benji winked at her. "But just a little bit still counts."

The sound of a baby's cries grew louder.

"Your *boppli*, Benji."

"Right. Just think about what I said." Benjamin broke into a jog and disappeared into the hallway.

Leah rolled her eyes. "Benji doesn't know what he's talking about," she said to Abby. "Now, let's forget about all that nonsense and see what we can whip up for dinner real quick."

Leah managed to get supper on the table, but it was not the big meal she had hoped to prepare. When Benjamin trotted back downstairs with his baby twenty minutes later, Leah was slathering peanut butter church spread on thick slices of yesterday's home-baked bread. Abby lay in her car seat on the butcher block counter, and Leah had to pause whatever she was doing every few seconds to rock the plastic carrier. For the first time, Leah understood why *Englischers* had fancy baby swings that rocked on battery power.

"No hot supper tonight, huh?" Benjamin asked.

Leah shot him a look just as Emma swept into the room carrying a jar of nutmeg. "Sorry it took me so long. Viola Esch was visiting Amos and Edna, and you know how that goes."

Leah knew exactly how that went. The elderly woman was the local busybody and would not allow anyone out of her sight until she had squeezed all the latest news from them.

"You didn't tell her about Abby and John, did you?"

Emma laughed. "You know I didn't have a choice."

"She'll be over here soon to meddle."

"I'm sure she will," Emma said.

"I suppose Amos and Edna would have mentioned it if you didn't," Leah said as she tapped the car seat again to keep it rocking, then slapped another slice of bread on the serving platter.

"For certain sure," Emma said. "A mystery baby on our doorstep? That's a story that will spread like wildfire."

The front door opened, and the sound of voices and footsteps filled the entry hall. Leah frowned. She had not even finished making the open-faced sandwiches, much less managed a side salad. Or *any* side, for that matter.

Miriam, Amanda and Naomi filed into the kitchen and immediately began pulling dishes and glasses out of the cabinets. "I'm starving," Amanda said as she grabbed cutlery from the drawer.

Emma leaned in to Leah. "I'll slice some apples real quick, while Benjamin holds our baby. And I think there's some leftover potato salad in the fridge."

"*Ach*, thanks, Emma," Leah said before pivoting for the refrigerator.

"I know what it's like to have a *boppli* that you can't put down," Emma said. "I don't know what I'd do without Benji to help." She gave Leah a quick squeeze on the arm before hurrying to the fruit basket.

The kitchen was filled with the murmur of women's voices and the clatter and clang of silverware and porcelain as the sisters set the table and Benjamin paced the floor with a fussy baby in his arms.

"Let's eat," Leah announced as soon as the table was laid. The family scrambled into their chairs as she set the serving platter down beside a bottle of goat milk in the center of the big wooden table. Benjamin slid into his seat carefully, Caleb still in his arms. Leah carried Abby's car seat to the table and set it on the floor beside her, where she could keep rocking it with her foot.

Miriam did not waste any time. As soon as they had said grace, she raised her eyebrows and said, "Bread and peanut butter church spread? Not as easy as you thought it would be to keep the *boppli*, ain't so?"

"There's potato salad too," Leah said.

"I made that yesterday," Naomi said.

"Humph."

A knock on the door interrupted them.

"What now?" Leah muttered.

"The *daed* of that *boppli*, I imagine," Miriam said.

"*Ya*. I know. It's just..." Leah stopped herself. She was so tired that she had almost admitted that John annoyed her. And yet, something about him made her want to see more of him, which made her even more annoyed. She could not put her finger on what it was. But it didn't matter anyway. She refused to feel any interest for a man, especially an *Englischer*.

"Just what?" Amanda asked.

"Nothing."

"Are you going to answer the door?" Miriam asked.

For some strange reason, Leah felt a funny flutter in her belly knowing that John was there. It must be hunger. She scooped up a big spoonful of potato salad and plopped it on her plate. "*Nee*. I can't stop rocking this *boppli* or she'll cry."

"Benji, will you go?" Miriam asked.

"*Kumme* in!" Benjamin shouted. His baby stirred but didn't wake.

"I asked if you'd let him in, not holler across the house," Miriam said.

"*Ach*, as long as he comes in, it doesn't matter. Anyway, I can't put Caleb down." Benjamin took a big bite of bread with his free hand and chewed contentedly.

The front door creaked open slowly. "Hello?" John's voice asked. "Did you say to come in?"

Benjamin swallowed and wiped his mouth with his sleeve. *"Ya!"* he shouted. "We're in here."

There was the sound of heavy work boots sliding off, then thumping onto the hardwood floor of the entry hall. A moment later John padded into the room. He had dark circles under his eyes, and his brown hair was disheveled. His flannel shirt and jeans were stained with dirt. "How did she do?"

"She was *gut*," Leah said.

John leaned against the doorjamb. He looked like he couldn't force himself to stand up any longer.

"*Kumme* sit," Emma said.

"I don't want to impose," John said. His eyes moved to Leah's as if he were seeking permission, but she dropped her gaze.

"No imposition," Miriam said. "There's always room for one more." Then she gave Leah a sly smile. "Although there isn't much of a meal tonight. Leah was supposed to cook while we did the milking."

Leah shot Miriam a look. She knew that her sister was only teasing her, but it made her feel inadequate in front of John. Even though she did not care what he thought. Not one little bit. She was done caring about what men thought of her. Especially *Englisch* men.

John froze as his eyes landed on the serving platter, then he broke into a grin that crinkled the corner of his tired-looking eyes. "Is that peanut butter church spread?"

"Ya," Leah said.

"I can't resist the offer, then. It's been a long time since I've had any."

"Pull up a chair," Benjamin said. He took another big bite of bread, then nodded toward one of the heavy wooden chairs against the wall that they kept for guests.

"Thanks." John picked up a chair with one hand, as if it weighed nothing, and plunked it down beside Leah. She felt uncomfortable for him to sit so close. Her face must have shown it, because John quickly said, "So I can sit next to Abby."

"Of course," Leah murmured while staring at her plate. Why did she feel so hot and prickly when he was beside her?

"I hope Abby didn't give you too much trouble," John said as he reached for a big slice of bread.

"*Nee*, we had a *gut* time together."

Miriam laughed. "Now, Leah, don't you know better than to lie?"

A round of laughter passed around the table. John and Leah were the only ones who didn't laugh. He set the slice of bread onto his plate without taking a bite and turned to Leah with a frown on his face. "She cried?"

Leah tried not to look at John. His gaze was too piercing. It made her feel as if she had failed. She looked at her sister instead. "I didn't lie, Miriam." Leah raised her chin. "I said Abby didn't give me too much trouble. And she didn't."

"I'd like to hear your definition of too much trouble," Miriam said. Everyone laughed again, except for John and Leah.

"We did fine," Leah muttered. She was beginning to regret how hard she had worked to convince everyone that she didn't want to marry and have a family. Now no one thought she was capable of taking care of a baby. Sure, she had always been free-spirited, but that didn't mean she was incapable of responsibility. They had no idea how much her heart longed for this.

"Then why do you have baby powder all down the front of your dress?" Amanda asked. "And why does your *kapp* have a formula stain on it?" Naomi asked. "How did that happen?"

Leah felt a bolt of embarrassment shoot through her. She didn't want John to see her like this. Then she felt angry for caring.

"You can quit scowling, Leah," Benjamin said. "We're just joking. You did a *gut* job today. We all know it." He waited a beat before shooting a sly grin and adding, "Even if you didn't get the laundry or the cooking done. And even though you look like a complete mess."

"I'd like to see you get the milking done while holding a baby," Leah muttered.

"I couldn't," Benjamin said. "That's why Emma and I make a *gut* team." His and Emma's eyes met over the table, and they both smiled at one another. Sometimes those two could be so romantic it was irritating. Or maybe

Leah was just envious that they had something that she could not imagine having.

John shifted in his seat, and Leah wondered if Benjamin's words had made him uncomfortable too. Of course they had. He knew he was in this alone.

John leaned over and unbuckled Abby from the car seat.

"You shouldn't move her," Leah said. "She's finally happy. Don't mess with success."

"I need to hold her. I haven't seen her all day. She'll be fine."

"Don't count on it," Leah muttered.

Abby began wailing as soon as John lifted her. His face fell as he pressed her against his chest. She squirmed as she cried. "We'll go soon," John said.

"I told you so," Leah said.

"Thanks," John said in a flat tone. "That helps."

Leah knew she shouldn't have said it. She thought it would feel good, since he had disregarded her advice. But it didn't. She shoved a bite of potato salad in her mouth and looked away.

Abby kept wailing. John stood up and began to bounce her. He swayed, then stumbled and caught himself.

"Sit," Miriam said. "You're dead on your feet. I'll take her. Get some supper."

"I don't want to put her down," John said.

"You need to sit," Miriam said. "It's clear you didn't sleep last night. And you've been working construction all day, ain't so?"

"Yeah."

Miriam stood up and motioned for him to hand over the baby. "Sit," she said.

John sighed and nodded. "Thanks. I guess you're right.

I'm pretty bleary eyed." He passed Abby to Miriam, then dropped into his chair and stuffed a big bite of bread into his mouth. He chewed fast, then took another big bite. He swallowed and shook his head. "Leah, this is delicious. Best thing I've tasted in years."

"Oh." Leah straightened in her seat. "Really?"

John took another bite and nodded.

A mischievous smile tugged at Leah's lips. "So does it make up for me saying I told you so?"

John glanced over at her, and his eyes brightened for the first time since they'd met. "For certain sure." But as soon as the words were out of his mouth, he frowned and looked down at his plate. "I mean, yeah. Sure does."

John polished off five thick slices of bread, a big serving of potato salad and seven apple slices while the family chatted about their day and Miriam walked circles around the table, bouncing Abby. Leah poured herself a second glass of fresh milk, then looked over at John. He was fast asleep, sitting up. He looked so sweet with the frown lines gone from his forehead and the tension released from his shoulders. "Abby won't fall asleep, but her *daed* sure did," Leah said.

Everyone's attention turned to John.

"Poor thing," Emma said. "He can't work all day and stay up all night with that *boppli*."

Naomi shook her head. *"Nee."*

"He's going to need more help," Amanda said.

"There's nothing more we can do," Leah said. But something deep inside her heart tugged at her. She simply had to find a way to do more, no matter how much John got under her skin. For Abby's sake. And for the sake of her own secret dream to raise a baby.

The sound of horse hooves thudded in the distance.

Leah strained to hear better, then slumped back against her chair when she heard the crunch of buggy wheels against gravel. "She's just in time for dessert."

Emma laughed. "You were right. Viola never takes long to get the rest of the gossip. How would the Amish telegraph work without her?"

"Hey," Benjamin said. "If it weren't for Viola, Emma and I might not have gotten together. She was the one who played matchmaker, ain't so?"

Emma grinned. "She's the best matchmaker in Bluebird Hills."

"For certain sure," Benjamin said. "And," he added with a wink, "she lets herself in like she owns the place, so no one has to get up to answer the door."

Sure enough, they all heard Viola's cane tapping the hardwood floor three minutes later. "I'm here to see the new *boppli*," she said as she hobbled into the kitchen. "Someone fetch me a chair. And I'll take a slice of your pumpkin pie, Emma."

Emma giggled. "I haven't had time to make it yet. But Leah made gingerbread men yesterday. I'll get that."

"That'll do. I always—" Viola stopped short when she saw John slumped over, fast asleep. "This is the *Englisch daed*?"

"Ya," Emma said as she stood up to get the gingerbread and dessert plates.

Viola studied him through the bifocals balanced on the end of her nose and clucked her tongue. "Poor man. This won't do."

"We were just saying that," Amanda said.

"And I was just saying there's nothing we can do." Leah wanted to do more, but she did not want to see more of John than she already had to. She shouldn't be around an

Englischer who stirred up strange, unwanted emotions in her. The last time she felt this way was—Leah cut off the thought. She did *not* feel the same draw toward John that she had toward Steve. He had made her feel like she was standing at the edge of a cliff, heart pounding, palms sweating, ready to jump off the edge, not knowing if she would fall or fly. He had made her feel an addictive excitement she had never felt before. John made her feel... Well she didn't know how he made her feel. He had a soft way about him for such a big man. When he looked at Abby, she saw love in his eyes. Leah stopped herself from going any further with that thought. She had to keep her wits about her.

All she had to do was remind herself of the facts. John was like Steve. He didn't listen to her. He didn't respect her. Hadn't John just ignored her and done the exact opposite of what she had said to do? If he hadn't picked Abby up, the baby would still be content in her car seat. Serves him right that he's exhausted. Leah felt a little twinge of guilt at her reasoning but pushed it aside. Steve had fooled her. She would not be fooled again. She would notice the signs this time and keep her distance.

Viola tapped her cane against the table, where there was an empty space for her. "Could use a chair, young man."

"Right. Sorry." Benjamin started to get up, but Naomi put out her hand to stop him. "Don't wake up your son." She hopped up and dragged one of the extra chairs across the floor. John was sleeping so soundly that the noise didn't wake him.

Viola lowered herself onto the chair with a sigh. "Now, it's a *gut* thing I'm here, because I've already solved the problem."

"What problem?" Leah asked.

"Of this *Englischer daed*, of course."

Leah swallowed hard. She had a sinking feeling in the pit of her stomach that Viola's solution was going to force her down a path that she was afraid to take. But she also knew that she would do anything to keep Abby near.

John jolted awake. A surge of adrenaline shot through him before he realized where he was. "I, uh, I think I fell asleep. Sorry about that."

Everyone at the table laughed.

"You've been sleeping like the dead, young man," an elderly woman said. She had stark white hair and a skinny frame that hunched forward with age. He knew that he wasn't thinking straight after thirty-six hours without sleep—except for that unexpected nap—but he was sure that she had not been there earlier. John rubbed his eyes. "Hi. I'm John Mast."

"I know who you are," she said as she peered down at him from the bottom halves of her bifocals. Her voice was surprisingly strong for a woman who looked to be in her eighties or nineties.

"Right. Okay."

"Now, here's the solution."

"To what?" John asked.

"Your problem."

"Sorry, who are you?"

"Viola Esch." She waved her hand as if swatting a fly. "But that's not important right now. Let's stick to the subject."

"Which is?" John began to wonder how long he had been asleep. He seemed to have missed a lot.

"That you're moving to Stoneybrook Farm."

"What?" John shook his head, gave a nervous laugh. This was too bizarre. "I thought you said I'm…moving here?"

Viola rapped her cane against the hardwood floor. "That's exactly what I said."

"You didn't think to, you know, ask me?"

Viola looked upward, as if she couldn't bear the nonsense. "*Youngies* today," she muttered. "Don't know what's best for them."

John glanced around the table. Maybe poor Viola wasn't so sharp anymore. She could have dementia or something. But the Stoltzfus family were all looking rather smug, as if they were all in on it. Except for Leah. She looked as if she had swallowed something sour. John frowned. "I'm going to need a better explanation. What's going on here?"

Leah exhaled. "You can't go on like this."

"Like what?"

Leah raised an eyebrow. "You're obviously not getting any sleep. And then you have to work all day at a dangerous job."

"It's only been one night."

"And you really think tonight will be different?"

John didn't say anything. They both knew it would be the same. In fact, every night would probably go like last night for months to come. He rubbed his forehead. "Look, I appreciate the offer, but this is a little, well, ridiculous. I can't just move here." He studied Leah. "Besides, I'm pretty sure you don't want me here."

"That's irrelevant. I certain sure want your *boppli* here. She needs us, and I'm not going to let her down."

"But I'm just irrelevant." Of course he was.

Leah made a noise in the back of her throat. "That's not what I meant."

"Then what did you mean? Because that sounded pretty clear to me."

"It means that it doesn't matter if you're here," Leah said. "But Abby needs—"

"Right," John interrupted. "It doesn't matter if I'm—"

The sharp rap of Viola's cane on the floor interrupted John. "That's enough."

Miriam raised a hand. "What we're trying to say is—"

"I'm perfectly capable of saying what I want to say," Leah interrupted.

"Leah. Just let me explain this to him."

Leah threw up her hands, then slouched back in her chair. "Fine."

Miriam took a deep breath. "*Oll recht*. How long does it take you to get to work from here?"

"Uh, about an hour. It's clear across the county."

"Right. And where do you live?"

"I've got a studio apartment in the city of Lancaster."

"On a year's lease?"

"No. Just week to week."

"Perfect."

"Look, can you just tell me what this plan of yours is? Because none of this is making sense."

"What doesn't make sense is you driving four hours a day, back and forth, working all day, and then going home to take care of a *boppli* all alone," Viola said. "No one has the stamina for that."

"How long are your shifts?" Miriam asked.

"Twelve hours, usually."

"Okay. We've got work that needs to be done, right here on the farm. We've been wanting to add a room to the house since Emma moved in. You may have noticed that it's had additions in the past."

"I did." The rambling two-story building had caught his eye the first time he saw it. The original portion of the house was a big box with a double front porch—one on each floor—with asymmetrical additions tacked onto the side and back that made the home unique and interesting. It looked like a place where a big, boisterous family with lots of personality would live. "But you could have work frolic for that."

Miriam shook her head. "*Nee.* I wouldn't call on the community for this. It isn't a necessity. But it's something we'd like done. I know the house looks big, but there are a lot of us. And our family is growing fast."

Emma and Benjamin smiled at each other.

"You build houses, right?" Naomi asked.

"Yeah."

"Take care of this job for us in exchange for room, board, a little cash and help with your *boppli*," Miriam said. "You won't be on your own with her all night, every night, after working a twelve-hour day."

"That's a kind offer, but I really couldn't—"

"What you can't do is take care of this *boppli* by yourself," Viola cut in. "Babysitting isn't enough. You need an intervention."

"You need family," Miriam added gently.

John looked around the room. Every face stared back at him with a confident expression. He began to suspect that they had an ulterior motive. The Amish always wanted to see their own come back to the fold. "I don't have a family," he said.

"All Amish are family," Viola said.

His suspicion had been right. "I'm not Amish."

Viola and Miriam exchanged a meaningful glance.

"Let's not worry about that right now," Miriam said. "Just let us help you."

John puffed out his cheeks and exhaled. "I don't take charity."

"It's not charity. You'd be working."

He tried to think of a better excuse. Returning to the Amish—even just as a visitor—made him feel too uncomfortable. He wasn't ready to face his past and decide his future. His gaze swung to Leah. She was staring at him with those guarded brown eyes. He definitely wasn't ready to face her. How could he stand to see her every day, all day? She knew exactly how to get under his skin. In fact, she was so irritating that he hadn't been able to stop thinking about her since they met. Last night, as he paced the floor with Abby, his mind had kept wandering back to Leah, with her spray of freckles, the way she raised her chin when she defended herself—John cut off the thought. "It sounds too complicated," he said.

"Living on your own sounds much more complicated," Miriam said.

"Gut." Viola tapped her cane on the floor to emphasize the word. "Now that that's decided, let's go over the rules."

"I haven't agreed," John said.

Leah gave him a look. "It's best for Abby, ain't so?" She held his gaze. "We're putting her first, no matter how we feel."

He scratched his head, then threw up his hands. "Okay. You're right. It's best for Abby."

"I knew you were a sensible young man," Viola said. "Now, about those rules. You'll have to live as Amish."

John had expected that, but it didn't soften the blow. Living as Amish would not make him Amish. And everyone would know that. Could he bear to be the outsider?

He would have to. He nodded. "I wouldn't disrespect you by living as an *Englischer* while I'm here."

"That includes dressing as Amish," Miriam said.

John nodded. "I understand." His stomach was slowly sinking, even as he felt a warm wave of comfort at the thought of returning to what was safe and familiar. It was strange that he could feel both things at the same time.

"And can you two get along?" Benjamin asked. He gave Leah a mischievous grin.

"Of course we can," she shot back. "We're not *kinner*." But as she stared at John, her eyes flashed with an expression that said otherwise. She was clearly unsettled. Was she that put off by him? She must be. He had left the Amish, after all. Of course she would be wary. The others must be wary too.

So why was it that Leah's opinion mattered more to him than the rest? Better not to ask himself too many questions. That might lead to answers that he didn't want to hear. He had more than enough to worry about as it was.

Chapter Four

The community rallied so fast that John barely had time to doubt his decision. In fact, it felt less like a choice and more like being swept away with the current. Viola sent the word out on the Amish telegraph that there was a need for men's clothing, and several families donated spare pants, shirts, suspenders and a black felt winter hat and black winter coat. The pants were all too short for John's six-foot-four-inch frame, but Viola and Edna didn't let that slow down his return to the Amish. They pulled out their treadle sewing machines and, by the next morning, John had two pairs of brand-new, hand-sewn trousers that fit him—and fit the requirements of the local *Ordnung*. He was surprised when he dropped off Abby that morning to see a stack of neatly folded clothes waiting for him on the arm of the family's worn couch. The sight reminded him that he was not one of them. He hoped putting those clothes on didn't feel dishonest. Because right now, he wasn't sure he could live up to his end of the bargain to live as Amish.

He would wait to change into them until he returned. Better to put it off as long as possible. First, he had to settle things with his boss and his landlord. John hurried back across the county to his construction site. He offered to give a two-week notice, but his boss said it wasn't necessary. There were other men who needed the work and could start right away.

Packing his belongings took less than an hour. John only had the bare necessities. After he loaded the cardboard boxes into his car, he doubled back to his worksite and offered to lend a coworker—ex-coworker, now—his car. John wasn't ready to sell it yet. He couldn't be sure this ludicrous scheme was going to work out. Everything was moving too fast. And, he knew that his coworker needed a car but couldn't afford one. John told himself that the arrangement was for the best and that everything was working out, but doubt nibbled at the back of his mind.

An hour later, an *Englisch* driver dropped John off at the Stoltzfus farm. He felt strange riding with a driver, as if he were Amish, while still wearing his fancy clothing. The driver didn't ask any questions, and John was thankful for that. The *Englisch* kept themselves to themselves more often than not, in his experience.

When he arrived, the property looked empty. He stepped out of the car into the bright sunlight of the front yard, thanked the driver and began to pull boxes from the trunk. As soon as the last one hit the ground, he slammed the trunk shut and thumped the side of the car with his hand to send the driver on his way. The man waved at him in the rearview mirror and took off, leaving a trail of dust billowing up from the gravel driveway as the hum of the engine—and John's *Englisch* life—faded away.

John took a deep breath and picked up one of the boxes from the ground. He wondered where everyone was, and where he should unload his belongings. Then he heard a hiss, followed by the slap of feet across hard-packed earth. A goose erupted from behind the house, its long, snaky neck outstretched and its black eyes flashing. The bird homed in on John, honked and snapped its bill.

"Whoa, now," he said in his gentlest voice as he took a quick step back.

The goose did not listen. It continued to charge and hiss. John shifted the box in his hands to fill the space between them, like a shield. The goose cut the distance fast, honked and lunged for his leg. John jumped back, but still got nipped on the knee. "Ouch!" He dropped the box and his jeans and T-shirts spilled out across the muddy lawn.

The goose seemed delighted. It honked, flapped its wings and lunged again.

"Belinda!" Leah's voice called out from the front porch. The screen door slammed shut as her black athletic shoes thudded across the floorboards. "Hey! Stop that! He's a friend!" She clapped her hands to get the goose's attention as she sprinted down the steps and across the yard. "Stop!"

Belinda took another nip at John, then pulled back and swung her long, snaky neck to stare at Leah. "He belongs here now, ain't so?" Leah skidded to a stop, scooped up the goose and tucked her under her arm. "Now, quit that *nonsens*." Belinda ruffled her feathers and stared at John with glittering black eyes, but did not lunge at him.

"She doesn't mean any harm," Leah said.

John chuckled. "Oh, I think she does."

Leah smiled and patted Belinda's head with her free hand. "She's just doing her job. She's a *gut* guard goose."

"Yeah, she gave me a *gut* nip."

Leah flinched. "*Ach*, I'm sorry."

John flashed a quick grin. He knew what he was going to say and wanted to stop himself, but couldn't. Leah was too easy to tease. "That's okay, since you called me a friend. Now I know how you really feel about me."

"*Nee*, I didn't mean that—" Leah clapped her mouth shut and shook her head. "Wait, that didn't *kumme* out right. You're not a friend but, I mean…"

John smiled. "I know. I was just giving you a hard time. I don't expect us to be friends. But we can get along for Abby's sake."

"Right."

John crouched down and began shoving his clothing back into the cardboard box he had dropped.

"Here, let me help." Leah lowered Belinda onto the ground and let go. "Now, you leave John alone, *ya*?" Belinda hissed, flapped her wings and took off toward the goat pen. Leah brushed off her hands, then leaned over and reached for a T-shirt on the ground. John reached for it at the same time, and they both grabbed a sleeve. Leah laughed. "I've got it."

"It's okay, you don't have to help."

"*Vell*, I'm not going to leave you to pick this all up by yourself. Let go."

"Really, it's okay."

Leah tugged harder. "*Nee*, let go."

"Okay." John let go, but Leah was still pulling on the T-shirt. She lost her balance, gave a little squeak and began to fall backward. John shot forward and grabbed her by the forearms. "Gotcha."

She gasped, then froze for a moment. Their eyes locked. John felt a jolt zip through him as she stared up at him, her mouth slightly parted, her eyes wide with surprise. Leah broke the moment almost immediately. Her expression dropped into a frown, and she looked away. "I'm fine."

"*Ya*, you are now." John gave a little half smile. He let her go and stepped back. "Because of me."

Leah grunted.

John chuckled.

Belinda honked in the distance.

"You're not going to thank me?" John asked, still smiling.

Leah was not smiling. *"Danki,"* she muttered, then dropped to the ground to throw the rest of the clothes back into the box. John couldn't help but notice how cute she looked as she tried to maintain her dignity. He would have to tease her more often.

"You can store everything in the tack room of the barn," Leah said. "You won't need any of this stuff. But *kumme* inside and get changed first." John suddenly remembered that he wasn't one of them. His jeans and flannel shirt marked him as an outsider. And, he knew that even after he put on the outward appearance of an Amish man, he would still be *Englisch* on the inside, to the others, at least. As far as he was concerned, he wasn't either one. He couldn't remember the last time he knew who he really was.

Leah led John to a ground-floor room at the back of the house. "Our family has filled up all the bedrooms upstairs," Leah said as she pushed open the door with a slow creak. "We added this on a few years ago. It's pretty cramped, but it will do for a bedroom. There's just enough room for a crib beside the bed. We'll have to get one. Right now, Abby is napping with Caleb in his crib upstairs." A faded blue quilt lay atop the narrow mattress, and there was a kerosene lamp on an upside-down milk crate wedged into the corner beside the bed.

John nodded. "Okay, thanks."

John wasn't sure whether to feel safe or trapped when Leah slipped out of the room and the door clicked shut behind her. He liked the comfort of a small, snug room. The simplicity of the bare walls and sparse, practical furnishings reminded him of the bedroom he had slept in when he was young. Except now, the walls felt like they were closing in on him.

He moved to the window, pulled up the green shade that the Lancaster Amish used, then pushed open the window. It held fast for a moment before unsticking. The room must not have been used in a while, except for storage. A cold December breeze swept into the room, bringing in the scent of the barnyard and pine needles. John stared at his view for a moment. The backyard was tidy and empty, except for an industrial-looking building with bare walls and no windows. He figured it must be where the family stored and processed the goat milk. Beyond the building lay wide open pastureland that sloped upward in a dark green carpet. He could make out a herd of goats at the top of the hill, far in the distance. A pair of border collies circled the herd in slow, deliberate movements. The clang of bells and the bark of the Anatolian shepherd drifted on the breeze and into the room.

John forced himself to turn away from the window and get on with it. After he changed into his new Amish clothing, an uneasy wave of nostalgia swept over him as he adjusted the sleeve of his plain blue shirt. Slipping into those clothes was like sliding back into childhood. They brought back the smell of fresh baked bread and hot black coffee at church dinners, the warm, damp scent of mud and livestock, the flicker of yellow light from a candle flame. The memories clung to him along with the fabric, made him want to let go and sink back into the way he was raised.

But those were not the only memories. There were

also the hard, sharp looks of people in his district who had not approved of his parents. There were the whispers and shaking heads. And his mother's restless expression as she yearned for something more that she never seemed to find, even after they left. Or the clink of the whiskey bottle that his father drank from, even before they left, when the family had already begun to give up on the Amish way of life.

He pushed the memories aside and doubled back outside to put his belongings into the barn. He shooed away a chicken pecking the side of one of the cardboard boxes that he had left in the farmyard, then hoisted the stack into his arms.

The earthy smell of the barn took him back to childhood as soon as he walked inside. Sunlight shone through the cracks between the wall's unfinished wooden boards and cast yellow stripes across the concrete floor. Dust motes hung in the air and made him sneeze. He strode past the empty goat pens to the small room at the far end of the building. He chose a corner behind a battered work table and set down his cardboard boxes. He stared down at all his belongings. There wasn't a lot there. For someone who lived in the fancy *Englisch* world, he didn't have much to show for it.

He pulled out his cell phone. It felt so familiar and comforting against his palm. How would he manage to let go of this lifeline to the outside world? He had begun to take those connections for granted. Would he be able to handle the isolation without it? Leah's face came to mind. John frowned. She would be a terrible replacement for a cell phone. Sure, she would keep him occupied with her quips and put-downs, but that was not his idea of entertainment or connection. But at least he wouldn't be bored with her to goad him all the time.

John shook his head and sighed. For the hundredth time since Viola's announcement the night before, he asked himself what in the world he was doing. He pushed the doubt away for Abby's sake and opened the flap of a cardboard box. He was about to drop the phone on top of his folded T-shirts when it vibrated in his hand. He stopped and stared at the caller ID. East Valley Construction, Ohio. This was the job he had applied to a few weeks ago, in hopes of making a better life for himself. It was a good opportunity. Better pay, better hours, and a path to management, eventually. His heart jumped into his throat as he took the call.

"Hello?"

"Hi, is this John Mast?" a woman's voice asked.

"Yes."

"This is Kaitlin, at East Valley Construction. We want to offer you the job."

John wasn't sure how to react. Twenty-four hours ago, there would have been no question. He would have taken the job on the spot, packed his car and been in Ohio by the next day. But now?

He swallowed hard. "I, uh… Some things have changed…"

"Oh." Kaitlin sounded surprised. "We thought you were eager to work for us."

"I am," John said quickly. "But, well, I've got some complications now." He pinched the bridge of his nose with a thumb and finger as he tried to get the right words out. "Can you give me a little time to decide?"

There was a long, hard silence on the other end of the line. John's pulse tapped in against his temple. He needed this job. He should take it. How could he risk losing it?

But how could he risk the opportunity for Abby to get the support she needed? They wouldn't know anyone in Ohio. He would be starting over, once again.

"We need an answer as soon as you can give us one," Kaitlin said after a moment. "There aren't any other candidates we want to hire at the moment, so the job is going to stay open for now. That gives you some time." She sighed. "But we have to fill it before the New Year, okay? You need to let us know by the thirty-first."

"Okay. I will. I'm sorry about this."

"Just let us know. If we find anyone else to fill the job in the meantime, we'll have to give it to them."

"Right. Okay."

The call clicked off abruptly.

John exhaled. This was a complication he had not expected. Choices were good, in theory, but in real life, they made things harder. Now he had a deadline to decide whether to stay *Englisch* or return to the Amish. And he knew that whichever choice he made, it would set him on a permanent path. He wouldn't raise Abby in two different worlds. The confusion and disruption of going from one to the other was too hard. Once he decided what to do, he would stick with it, for good.

Now he had two weeks to make a decision that would set the course of both their lives, forever.

Leah tried not to stare when John walked into the kitchen. He had transformed into a traditional Amish man in a plain shirt that fastened with hooks and eyes instead of buttons, black broadfall trousers, a black felt hat and suspenders. But he still had the same aloof half smile on his face. He might look Amish, but in his heart, he was still *Englisch*. Leah would have to remember to keep that in mind. Otherwise, she might soften her resolve and let him get too close. There would be consequences for that. She studied the masculine lines of his strong jaw, pronounced brow and straight, Roman nose. He was too handsome for his own good.

Leah frowned and turned back to the dirty dishes in the big farmhouse-style sink.

John chuckled. "You look like you just drank sour milk. What's the matter? Don't like my new look?"

Leah stiffened. Was he on to her? Did he realize that she had just been thinking that he was handsome? No. That wasn't possible. Besides, she could recognize that a man was good-looking without being sweet on him. Those were two very different things. She was just observing him. That was all. She just wished that her heartbeat would slow down and agree with her logic.

Leah clucked her tongue. "Dressing plain isn't a 'look,' it's a way of life."

She heard John sigh behind her. "Right. Okay. So what work do you have for me to do? I'm ready to get started."

Leah realized that she had been too critical. Well, sometimes that was necessary to keep distance. But she couldn't help feeling a tinge of remorse. What would it be like to return to the Amish as an outcast, caught between two worlds? Not easy, that was certain sure. "Have you had anything to eat today?" She wouldn't apologize, but she could soften her stance.

She could feel John's presence behind her. He hesitated. The soapy dishwater sloshed against the side of the sink. She pulled her hands from the water and picked up the dish towel on the counter. *"Vell?"* she asked as she dried her hands. "Are you hungry or not?" She turned around to see John's expression. His jaw looked tight. His eyes were on the window, watching something far away.

"I've not eaten today," he said quietly. "But no need to go to any trouble. I'll be fine."

"Don't be silly. You need to eat." She tossed the dish towel on the counter. "A man as big and tall as you must need a lot of fuel."

"Yeah," he murmured. "I've heard that before."

"Because it's true."

"I guess so."

Leah had to crane her neck to meet his eyes, and when she did, the look behind them made her glance away quickly. John had a tough facade, but there was a vulnerability hidden inside that made her want to reach out and touch him.

That was ridiculous. He was an outsider. A stranger. Even though the bishop vouched for him, he had been away a long time. There was no telling what he was thinking or feeling. He was probably as hard on the inside as he looked on the outside. She needed to stay strong. She knew better than to make friends with arrogant *Englischers* who thought they knew best.

"There're leftover ham biscuits in the fridge," Leah said as she turned to the cabinet and opened one of the doors. She was careful to keep her voice unemotional and distant. "And pumpkin pie. Benjamin always eats dessert with breakfast." She pulled down a glass and handed it to John. "And there's always fresh goat milk, of course."

He stepped forward and reached for the glass. She didn't try to meet his eyes. Something about his height and closeness made her belly flutter. Then his hand closed around hers. She could feel the strength in his calloused palm and broad fingers. The fluttering turned into a jolt.

Leah pulled her hand back fast. "*Vell*, just help yourself." Her voice sounded funny. She cleared her throat and wiped her hands on her apron. "I've got work to do."

"Right. Don't let me distract you."

"You're not." She was probably just nervous about the exam she had to take for her business class. This feeling had nothing to do with John. She had been trying to study while Abby napped, but the dishes had to be done. And after that there were plenty of other chores on the to-do list, as always.

"Where is everyone else?" John asked.

Leah could hear him walking to the propane-powered refrigerator.

"Benjamin is up in the south pasture with the goats. My sisters are in the production building or in the barn, and Emma is upstairs with the *bopplin*."

The refrigerator opened and glass clinked. Leah did not turn around to look. She tried to focus on the textbook on the counter that she had been reading while scrubbing a casserole dish.

"For such a big family, it's quiet around here." The refrigerator door shut with a muffled thump.

"Just wait until the *bopplin* wake up. It won't be quiet then. Or when Benjamin *kummes* home. He's as loud as the *kinner*."

John chuckled. "*Ya*, I know how loud Abby can be." The kitchen chair scraped against the floor and porcelain thudded against wood. Leah didn't turn around. She tried to pretend that John wasn't there, but his presence was all she could think about. She reread a line in her textbook for the third time. Somehow, she wasn't processing it.

"What are you reading?"

Leah jumped. John was right behind her, staring down at her textbook.

"I thought you were at the table! You just scared me half to death!"

"Oh, sorry." He took a quick step back and nodded toward the cabinet. "I needed to get a plate."

Leah exhaled. Why was she so flighty around him? "*Ya*, of course. I didn't think about that. The cabinet on the left." She shifted toward the sink so that he could move around her. He was tall enough that he didn't have to reach up for the shelf. He paused after he pulled down a plate to stare at the textbook. "You haven't answered my question."

"*Ach*, it's nothing. Just some reading for a class I'm taking." Leah heard the defensiveness in her voice. "I know it's unusual."

John glanced at her, then back at the book. "Unusual isn't bad."

"Oh." Leah tried to focus on the casserole dish that she was scrubbing. "Most folks think so."

John shrugged and flashed a grin. "Guess I'm not most folks."

Leah cut her eyes to him. "You mean you're not Amish."

John's face fell. "I just meant that it's okay to learn about the world, if that's what you want to do."

"I'm not learning about the world, just about business. For the farm." Leah could hear the edge in her voice but couldn't stop herself. For some reason she felt hot and defensive. "So that we can make a better profit. It's tough making it as a small family farm. We need all the help we can get."

"Yeah, I get that. Not everything about me is worldly, okay? I didn't mean you should learn about the world in a bad way. I just meant that you shouldn't be afraid of discovering the truth about what's around you. If God made it, then why be scared to find out about it? Don't you think God can handle it if we want to know more about the way things work?" John shook his head. "You know what? Never mind. I'll take my breakfast and my worldly *Englisch* ways out to the front porch, before I corrupt you."

Leah threw down the dishrag in her hand. It hit the water hard and soap suds splashed her apron and face. She wiped her eye as she spun around. "I didn't mean..."

But it was too late. John was striding out the kitchen door with a ham biscuit in one hand and a jug of milk in the other.

Chapter Five

John wolfed down the ham biscuit while standing on the front porch. A light dusting of snow drifted down from heavy gray clouds. While he chewed, John watched the chickens peck the ground as the bare earth slowly turned white. The flurries slowed to a stop and more chickens scurried out of the coop, clucking and flapping their wings. John's eyes moved beyond the wooden fence, past a long, gentle hill to where he could just make out a shimmer of water surrounded by a bare field. Soon, the water would freeze over. He squinted as he took another bite. Was that the field where Bishop Amos used to grow sunflowers in front of a pond? He had a vague memory of swimming in a pond behind Amos and Edna's house when he was a child. Afterward, he and some friends had run through the rows of blossoms. The flowers had been taller than they were, making it the best place for hide-and-seek he'd ever seen.

John swallowed his last bite, then smiled at the memory as he brushed the biscuit crumbs from his hands. Childhood had been good here, in the countryside, surrounded by folks he had known all his life, families he could depend on.

Until they turned on him.

John's smile disappeared. There was no use being sentimental. Life was more complicated than a handful of happy memories. He glanced back at the farmhouse window. A dark silhouette moved behind the glass, alongside the sound of a clanging dish. John looked away quickly. He had heard enough from Leah today. She had made herself clear. He was not about to go back in there and ask her for instructions. There was always something needing to be done on a farm. He would just figure it out on his own.

He took the porch steps two at a time, landed hard on the ground and strode over to the goat barn. He shifted his weight to one foot and studied the unpainted, weathered structure. It wasn't red like the barns in *Englisch* movies, but it had a good, sturdy look that felt old-fashioned and right, somehow. Except that there were some broken boards in a section near the ground. He crouched down and pushed one of the wooden boards. Rotten. He scanned the line where the building touched the damp earth. Too much moisture. These boards needed replacing.

Well, that was something he could do, especially now that the weather had cleared. His first instinct was to check his cell phone to see if it would start snowing again. He reached for his pocket before he remembered that he had no pockets in his broadfall trousers and no phone. He glanced at the sky. The clouds were breaking up, so hopefully he would be able to get the work done. Cold weather could be a good time for construction. The temperature was dropping faster than he'd like though. He blew on his hands, then rubbed them together.

John wondered if he should ask Leah if they had any tools or lumber, but decided that was the last thing he wanted to do. Instead, he searched the barn until he found what he needed. It took him longer than it would have if he had just asked, but it saved him another awkward conversation.

By lunchtime, his stomach was growling and his back was aching from crouching, but the job was done. He stood up, stretched and gave a satisfied nod. Then he tossed his hammer in the air, so that it flipped around in a full circle, and caught it by the handle with a smile. He had always been good at construction work, and he liked feeling useful.

"Playing around?" It was Leah's voice.

John's smile dropped to a frown as he turned around. "Got those rotten boards replaced for you."

Leah put her hands on her hips and scanned the work. John knew that there was nothing she could criticize. "I didn't ask you to do that."

And yet, she still found a way.

John raised his chin a little and looked down at her. She was so much smaller than him that it was impossible for her to be intimidating, even though she seemed to be giving it her best shot. "No, but it needed doing."

"We were saving those boards for the new addition on the house."

"Well, the barn needed them more. You can't let the wood rot like that. It's a real problem."

"It looked fine to me."

"Then you're part of the problem." John could feel the tension rising, so he flashed a disarming smile. "Good thing I came along when I did or you'd be in real trouble here."

"I am not a problem."

John kept the smile on his face. "Not an entire problem, just part of one."

Leah rolled her eyes. John was pretty sure she was

about to crack a smile too. Or maybe she was going to yell at him. It was hard to tell. Maybe he hadn't done such a good job easing the tension.

"Look, I just came out to tell you lunch is ready."

"Okay. Lunch is ready. Got it." John tossed his hammer again, but this time, he fumbled the catch and it slipped from his hand and hit the ground. Of course it did. John was not grinning anymore. Instead, he could feel a hot flush of embarrassment creep up from the collar of his shirt to color his face.

A slow, smug smile appeared on Leah's face. "'Pride goeth before destruction, and an haughty spirit before a fall.'"

John sighed, bent down to retrieve the hammer and straightened back up. "You enjoyed that fall, huh?"

"Immensely. Now *kumme* and eat." She turned around with a quick swish of her purple dress and marched back toward the house.

John was watching her walk away when Benjamin appeared around the side of the barn. "The work looks *gut*," he said, then chuckled. "No matter what Leah says."

"You heard all that?"

"*Ya*. Noise travels right though these walls. You know, we always give each other a hard time in this family, but outsiders aren't always used to it." He scratched the back of his neck. "*Vell*, to be honest, I guess she doesn't usually talk to outsiders like that."

John noticed that Benjamin used the word outsider to describe him but let it go. There was no reason to point it out. He knew how they felt about him, and nothing would change that.

"Just me," John said.

Benjamin flinched.

"First time for everything, I guess," John added when Benjamin didn't respond.

"*Ya.* And I didn't mean..." Benjamin took off his straw hat, raked his fingers through his hair and put it back on again. "I'm not so *gut* with words. And I know Leah means well. She's just..." Benjamin's brow crinkled as he searched for the right word.

"Don't worry about it."

"Danki." Benjamin nodded toward the house. "Now let's see what Leah and Emma have made for lunch. I'm starving."

The women had set the dining room table for the meal, instead of using the eat-in kitchen. The spacious room was lined with tall farmhouse windows. A wooden sideboard filled with an extra set of mismatched dishes sat against the opposite wall. There were red and green place mats beneath each plate, and an arrangement of holly and pine boughs lay across the center of the table, bordered by platters of fresh baked bread, peanut butter church spread, cold sliced ham, fruit salad, potato salad and iced sugar cookies in the shape of bells and stars. The smell of wood smoke drifted into the room to mingle with the scent of pine and fresh baked goods.

Naomi and Amanda arrived from the production building right behind John and Benjamin. John reached for a delicious-looking slice of bread still warm from the oven as everyone hurried into a chair. "Don't forget to pray over the meal," Miriam said as she strode into the dining room carrying a bottle of fresh goat milk in each hand. John froze. He had forgotten to say grace. It wasn't that he didn't believe in God. He talked to God quite a bit, but it was more conversational. He had forgotten the formalities of a more organized approach to religion. But of course, no one here knew that he enjoyed talking to God throughout his day. They must assume that he had no religion at all. He squeezed his eyes shut and asked God to help him fit in as they all prayed silently. Then Miriam cleared her throat to signal that the silent prayer time was over, and the family attacked the serving dishes. The food disappeared from the bowls and platters in a clatter of porcelain and silverware. Amanda and Leah tussled over who got the last spoonful of potato salad, and Benjamin used the distraction to sneak the last two sugar cookies onto his plate.

"Hey!" Leah said after Miriam told her sisters to split that final spoonful of potato salad. "Benji just took all the cookies!"

This time Miriam didn't intervene. Instead, she took a big bite of her open-faced ham sandwich and rolled her eyes.

"Give me one of those cookies," Leah said to Benjamin.

"You've already got one," he said.

"*Ya*, but you've got two, and that's not fair."

Benjamin gave an exaggerated shrug and grinned. "Life isn't fair."

"Your life isn't going to be fair after I get you back for this," Leah said.

Benjamin laughed. "Challenge accepted."

Leah tried to scowl at him but broke into a smile. "You have a talent for being annoying, Benji."

"I work hard at it, Leah. I'm glad you appreciate it."

Everyone laughed but John. He wasn't used to being at a table with such a close-knit family. His family had never joked or teased one another like this. If they had gone after each other the way Leah and Benjamin just had, it would have felt too genuine. It would have escalated into a fight, or turned into simmering resentment. But Leah and Benjamin were grinning at one another as they ate. "Mmm, these cookies sure are *abbeditlich*," Benjamin said as he stared at Leah with a glint in his eye.

"Benji, you ought to quit while you're ahead," Emma said as she smiled and shook her head.

"He'll never be ahead of me," Leah said. She winked at Emma, then turned to Benjamin as he chewed a big bite of sugar cookie. "You know, I've been debating what to make for dinner tonight, and I suddenly feel inspired to cook meat loaf. With extra ketchup."

Benjamin swallowed fast. "I hate ketchup!"

Leah smiled like a cat who had just gotten into the cream. "I know."

John ate quietly as the family chatted and teased one another. The babies slept in baskets on the floor as the family ate. John watched Abby as she breathed softly. One of her tiny hands was curled beneath her chin, and her lip twitched as she dreamed. He longed to pick her up, but he had learned his lesson the last time he did that while she was sleeping.

"John?"

Miriam's voice brought John's attention back to the table.

"I was asking if you've started on the new addition yet, since the weather cleared up."

"Uh, no. I wasn't sure…" He glanced at Leah. She had stopped eating, and her eyes dropped down to her lap. He decided not to tell on her. "I decided it was best to make some repairs on the barn first. I think Leah is planning on going over the plans for the new addition with me after lunch."

"Oll recht," Miriam said.

Leah's attention shot up to John. He winked fast, without anyone else noticing, since they were all looking at Miriam. Leah blushed and looked away again.

Caleb whimpered from his basket, then his eyes opened and his whimper turned into a full-blown cry.

Emma and Benjamin stood up at the same time. "I'll take him for a minute, before I have to go back to work," Benjamin said. He put a hand on Emma's shoulder. She covered his hand with hers, stood up on her tiptoes and kissed his cheek. He grinned and blushed as he walked past her.

Abby's eyes opened, and she stared at Caleb for an instant, then imitated him with an earth-shattering wail. Miriam pushed her chair back and smiled. "Break's over." John hurried over to his daughter, lifted her into the air and grinned at her. Her cries sputtered out as she stared down at him. He spun her slowly in the air. The snow had started up again outside the window, creating a soft, white backdrop that felt like Christmas. He told himself to take a picture of this moment in his mind. It would not last, no matter how much he wanted it to.

John stopped the thought. Did he really want this moment to last? Of course he did. Abby's babyhood was short and precious. These months would fly by. But he sensed that this feeling was about a lot more than that. Did he long for more meals like this one, where he was part of a family that laughed and joked and loved one another in a casual, unquestioning way? Did he long to be a part of the Stoltzfus family—a part of the Amish—for good?

John frowned and lowered Abby to his chest. She squirmed and gurgled as he held her close. There was no use in wanting what he could not have. The community had been welcoming, but he suspected their encouragement was only surface deep. Underneath the smiles, they would never let him in. Leah certainly wouldn't. And most people in the district would feel the same way.

Miriam stood and began stacking plates. "Leah, I'll clean up while you show John what we want done, *ya*?"

"I'll help you while Benji holds the baby," Emma said to Miriam. John held Abby close as he followed Leah outside to the side yard. The sun broke through the clouds as the flurries died down, and a soft breeze ruffled the strings of Leah's *kapp*. It would have been a lovely afternoon, if it weren't for the cold temperature and the expression on Leah's face. She sighed and looked away. "Thanks for covering for me."

"It's not a big deal."

"*Nee*, it kind of is. Miriam took the place of my parents after they died, and sometimes she takes the role too seriously. But I can't say anything because she's given up so much for the rest of us."

John nodded. He gave her steady eye contact to let her know that he was listening. But he didn't want to shut her down by saying anything. He could hardly believe that she was speaking to him at all, much less about something so personal.

"So, if you had told her that I left you on your own this morning..." Leah's gaze moved over to the Yoders' pond at the bottom of the hill, sparkling in the distance. "She would have had a lot to say about it."

"Ya." John couldn't believe that word had slipped out. There was something about Leah opening up to him that made him revert back to the familiarity of childhood. "I mean, yeah, that makes sense. And I'm sorry about your

parents. I remember when the accident happened. We all heard about it over in Little Creek."

"It was a long time ago," Leah said softly.

"People say time heals all wounds, but I haven't found that to be true."

Leah's eyes shot up to John. "You're right. Time just makes things…different. The grief gets softer, dimmer. But the consequences are still there. We're still living with those. We always will."

"Yeah. I understand that." John swallowed as he debated whether to say more. His heart rocketed up a notch as he decided to plunge forward. "I, uh, know that *Gott* gets us through it though. He doesn't take away the loss, but He's with us while we suffer."

Leah's brow crinkled. "Your parents are still alive, right?"

John nodded. "But I've lost them, all the same."

"Oh." Leah studied his expression in a long, unexpected moment of connection, then turned away.

John's heart was still beating too fast. And now his palms were sweating too. He had said too much. But he wasn't sorry. He had a feeling that Leah needed to hear what he had said. That made it worth it, even if he had embarrassed himself.

"I'm sorry," Leah said.

"You are?" John had not meant to let his surprise slip out like that.

Leah gave a wry laugh. "*Ya.* I should have made you feel more *willkumm* this morning." She hesitated. "So, you still believe in *Gott*?"

"For sure."

"Oh."

"You're surprised." John said it as a statement, not a question.

"I, uh, I don't know."

"Just because my parents left the Amish doesn't mean I stopped believing in *Gott.* I just stopped keeping the *Ordnung.*"

"Do you go to an *Englisch* church?"

John readjusted Abby's weight in his arms. "No."

"Why not?"

"I never belonged there. I never..." John was about to say that he never belonged anywhere. But he stopped himself. This conversation was getting uncomfortably intimate. He should have never let it go this far. What had gotten into the two of them? "You know, just because I don't live as Amish doesn't mean I'm a bad guy." John let his tone sharpen as he said the words. He could feel himself putting up a wall between them, but it was like watching someone else pushing her away. He wasn't even sure why he was doing it. He just knew that he felt too exposed to keep talking.

Leah stiffened. "*Recht*. Okay. I never said that."

"You sure have acted like it."

Leah's expression tightened. "You know what? Never mind. Forget I said anything at all."

"Got it. And you can forget I said anything too." John had a vague sense of shame that he was acting like an embarrassed child, but he pushed the feeling away.

"I will," Leah said, her voice just as sharp as his.

"Good. Glad we got that straight."

"Gut." Leah spun around and began to march across the lawn, toward the house.

"Hey, Leah," John called after her.

"What?" she asked without turning around.

"Aren't you going to show me what needs to be done on the house?"

Leah stopped, but she didn't turn around. Her shoulders were hunched, her body tight. She let out a noise that sounded like a cross between a sigh and a grunt. "Fine."

John wished he could tell her that he was sorry and that he wanted to hear more about her life, her childhood, her complicated relationship with her oldest sister. But he said nothing. He did not know how to bridge that gap between them.

Leah did not want to think about the awkward encounter she had had with John earlier that day. But she could not get him out of her mind as she hunched over the wringer washer on the enclosed back porch. Why had she told him about the tension between her and Miriam? Why had she mentioned her parents? What was it about him that made her want to open up?

Whatever it was, she had managed to do a pretty good job of doing the opposite. She had been pushing him away all day. Well, except for that embarrassing moment of weakness after lunch. What had gotten into her? She knew better than to open up to a man. Especially an *Englisch* man, even if he did use to be Amish. The fact that he hadn't returned to the faith just proved that she was right—he couldn't be trusted. Leah scowled and turned the crank harder.

She heard a shout and looked up through the wall of windows to see Benjamin striding down the hill with Ollie trotting beside him. She leaned forward and pulled open the door. A blast of cool air whipped inside. "Hey, Benji," she shouted back. He grinned as he trotted the rest of the way down the hill and up the porch steps. "Where's

John?" he asked as soon as he was inside. "You two decided to step out together yet?"

"Shhhh! He's right there, around the side of the house." She nodded around the corner of the old weathered building while she kept turning the hand crank. "Shut the door."

Benjamin closed the door with a bang before plopping down onto one of the wooden rocking chairs that lined the porch. Ollie turned a circle and dropped to the floor beside his feet. Benjamin leaned over and absentmindedly patted the dog's head.

"What are you doing?" Leah asked.

"I came to get a mug of hot chocolate, but thought I'd take a minute to bother you while I'm here."

Leah laughed. "Fine. But get me one too."

Benjamin bounced up and disappeared into the farmhouse with a slam of the screen door. No one had taken it down when they enclosed the porch, even though it wasn't necessary anymore. Leah wiped her forehead with her sleeve as she listened to the bang of John's hammer in the distance. She wondered what he was thinking while he worked. Not that she cared. A few minutes later, the screen door swung open and Benjamin walked out with a mug of hot chocolate in each hand, Ollie trailing behind him.

Leah stood up from the three-legged stool and stretched her back. "Thanks, Benji."

He held out one of the mugs to her before he sat down. "Now you have to answer a question to repay me."

Leah rolled her eyes as she took the hot chocolate from him, but she couldn't keep a smile off her face. She let out a long breath and sank onto a rocking chair beside him. "I'm worn-out."

"I'll help you hang the laundry before I do the evening chores," Benjamin said. "I know how heavy those wet blankets are. And shouldn't you be studying right now, anyway?"

"*Ya*. But I've got to get this laundry done while Emma's able to watch both the *bopplin*. So yeah, I could use the help. *Danki*."

"So now you owe me answers to two questions."

Leah laughed and gave her twin brother a little shove.

"Ouch," he said.

"That didn't hurt."

"Maybe you don't know your own strength."

"Ha ha, very funny. Now, what are your questions?"

"Right." Benjamin flashed a sly grin. "Why are you being so standoffish to John?"

"Your expression looks like you think you already know the answer."

"I do. But I want to hear you say it."

Leah glanced at the corner of the house. "Just keep your voice down, *oll recht*?"

"Because you want to keep this conversation secret from John?"

"*Nee*. *Vell*, I mean yes. But not because—Benji, just let me talk, okay?"

"I don't think I'm stopping you." Benjamin gave her an innocent smile, then took a sip of his hot chocolate. A cardinal flew across the yard and landed in the bare branches of the oak tree. The dusting of white snow clinging to the bark contrasted against the red feathers.

"I'm not being standoffish toward him," Leah said in a low voice.

"*Nee?* Just being mean, then?"

Leah shot Benjamin a look. *"Nee."*

"*Vell*, you're not being very nice."

Leah puffed out her cheeks, then let out the air in a rush. "You ask too many questions."

Benjamin raised an eyebrow. "They shouldn't be hard to answer."

"I'm not sweet on him."

"Uh-huh. Keep telling yourself that and maybe you'll believe it eventually."

Leah couldn't manage a laugh. She held both hands against her mug. The warm porcelain felt good against her skin. Neither of them spoke for a moment. Leah became even more aware of the construction sounds coming from the side yard. "You know I'm not interested in courting anyone. I've got a plan. Finish my business classes, manage the finances around here, just be free a while longer. You know I don't want to end up like Miriam. Not yet, anyway. I need more time before I have to be responsible for a family. If I ever do have one."

"Whoa, so now you're thinking about marrying him?"

"What? *Nee!* I just said I didn't want to marry anyone. Not for a long time."

"But you're thinking about marriage and you're thinking about him, so..." Benjamin shot her a sly grin.

"You're not funny, Benjamin."

Her brother kept smiling to himself. He sipped his hot chocolate, then wiped his mouth on his sleeve. "You sure you're not making excuses?"

Leah snorted. "What do you mean, making excuses? That's ridiculous. You know how much I like taking those classes. And you know how important it is that we all pull our weight around here. And why shouldn't I get a chance to travel someday?"

"Uh-huh. Right." Benjamin cleared his throat. "You used to talk about wanting to get married and having children, and then one day, all the sudden, you said you never would. It's pretty obvious something happened. You haven't been the same since your *Rumspringa*."

"Maybe I grew up and realized what I wanted in life."

"Or maybe something happened." Benjamin lowered his voice. "Maybe you got your heart broken?"

"Pffft." Leah crossed her arms and looked away.

"*Ya*. I thought so. I'm sorry, Leah."

"I didn't get my heart broken."

Benjamin didn't say anything for a while. The rocking chairs creaked as they moved in silence.

"It isn't like you to treat someone this way," Benjamin said after a while.

"You think I'm being too hard on him?"

"For certain sure."

Leah's mouth tightened.

"I would expect it from one of our sisters, but not from you," Benjamin said.

"They're just overprotective."

"*Ya*, I know. And neither one of us like it when they are. So why are you acting that way?"

"I'm not protecting John."

"*Nee*, that's not what I meant. You're protecting yourself." Benjamin glanced at Leah. "Ain't so?"

Leah stared out the wall of windows, past the red cardinal, to the pastureland beyond. "I'm not going to answer that."

"So, you do like him."

"I never said that." Leah hesitated. She raised her mug to her mouth, then lowered it before she took a sip. "But we did have a strange conversation today. We kind of... connected, I guess." She shook her head. "Never mind. It's silly."

"I doubt that," Benjamin said.

Leah clucked her tongue. "*Nee*, it's nothing. And it doesn't matter anyway. We don't get along. He's too *Englisch*."

"And he'll stay that way if you keep making him feel unwelcome here."

Leah flinched. Was Benjamin right about that? She stood up fast, then shoved her mug into Benjamin's hand. "I've got to get back to work."

"You've barely drank any hot chocolate."

"More for you then."

Benjamin gave her a funny look. "*Ya*, I'll finish it for you no problem, but…" His eyes narrowed. "Why don't you just relax and be yourself, *oll recht*?"

"It's more complicated than that," Leah snapped. She stalked over to the wringer washer and dropped onto the three-legged stool.

"Is it?" Benjamin looked like he already knew the answer to that.

"Look, we shouldn't go easy on him. John needs to know that it's not okay to leave the Amish. What if he decides to go back to the *Englisch* and take Abby with him? What if he raises her to be fancy and worldly?" Leah knew how easily someone who seemed like a good man could prove otherwise. She couldn't afford to give John the benefit of the doubt.

"This isn't the way to bring him back to the faith, Leah. You're only going to convince him to leave. And he'll take Abby with him." Benjamin studied her for a moment. "And why are you so worried about that, anyway?"

"Because of Abby, of course."

"I thought you didn't want to settle down and have children, remember?"

"I don't want the husband that comes with the children!" Leah clamped a hand over her mouth. She had not meant to say that part out loud, but her emotions had overflowed. Benjamin could have that effect on her.

Benjamin's eyes and voice softened. "You were seeing an *Englischer* last year, weren't you? When you started acting funny during your *Rumspringa*—right before you started saying you'd never get married."

"Do you really think I'd do something that foolish?"

"We all make mistakes."

Leah exhaled. "Let's say, theoretically, that I did."

"Right." Benjamin narrowed his eyes. "Theoretically."

"Then I would never fall for another *Englischer* again, that's for certain sure."

"So this isn't just about Abby," Benjamin said.

"Of course it is. I told you, I'm not interested in courting anyone, especially an *Englischer*. It's preposterous."

"Right. Preposterous." Benjamin gave Leah a look.

"Preposterous," Leah repeated.

"What's preposterous?" John's voice rang out as the porch door swung open.

"Nothing!" Leah said more forcefully than she should have.

"Right. Okay." John stomped his boots on the doormat before stepping inside. Benjamin chuckled quietly and took another sip of hot chocolate.

Leah could feel her face heating up. How much had John overheard? She bent down, pulled a white pillow case from the wringer, tossed it in the laundry basket and started to pick it up. She grunted as she strained to lift the basket full of heavy, wet linens. Footsteps thudded behind her, then John whisked the basket from her hands. "I got it," he said.

"*Nee*, I've got it."

John sighed as he hoisted the basket higher and trotted across the porch and down the steps. "Look, I don't want to fight. But I'm not going to stand by while you struggle to carry this."

Leah swallowed hard as she watched him. He carried the basket as if it weighed nothing. And it looked comically small in his big, calloused hands. His blue shirtsleeves were rolled up to the elbows, despite the cold, and she tried not to stare at the hard outlines of the muscles that rippled beneath his bare forearms.

Benjamin chuckled and stood up. "I'm going to check on Emma and the *boppli*."

"You said you were going to help me with the laundry."

Benjamin winked. "You don't need it anymore."

Leah glared at him. She needed more help than ever. But not with the laundry. With something much more complicated.

Chapter Six

John spent his first night at Stoneybrook Farm tossing and turning on the narrow bed. His legs were too long for the mattress and his feet hung off the edge. Every time he rolled over, the old box springs creaked beneath his weight. But it wasn't the bed that kept him awake. It was the dread of the next morning, because it would be a church Sunday. When he finally did drift off to sleep, he jerked awake a moment later, heart racing, his breath caught in his throat. He couldn't remember his dream, but it pulsed through his veins, reminding him that nothing would be okay.

John took a deep breath and let it out slowly. He sat up and swung his legs onto the floor. Outside the window, the rolling hills were dusted white in the moonlight. A few flurries drifted down, soft and silent as goose down. Above him, on the second floor, the Stoltzfus family slept peacefully. He glanced down at Abby, who lay in a bassinet beside the bed. She was sleeping too. Her sweet face looked peaceful while she made little sucking motions with her mouth, as if she were drinking from her bottle.

How could he feel so alone while surrounded by people? John began to speak out loud, to the only one he knew would always be there, regardless of how alone he felt.

"I'm not sure I've done the right thing, *Gott*." John moved his eyes from Abby back to the window. Clouds skidded across an inky black sky to cover the moon, blocking the light and dimming the room. "I don't know if I'm supposed to be here right now. It feels so right and so wrong at the same time." The clouds floated past the moon and silver light reappeared to cast a glow across the dark room. An owl hooted from somewhere in the distance. "How can I face all those folks tomorrow? What will they think of me?" John sighed. "I don't know how to put it into words. Just please make everything right for Abby and me. Show me what to do. I've got this job offer, and it's a really good opportunity…" His voice trailed off and he sighed again. There was nothing to do now but trust that his prayer would be answered. Waiting was harder than acting. He wished he could do something.

Well, tomorrow he would. He would go to the church service in the district and see how he felt there. The knot in his stomach told him it would not go well. But he wanted to believe otherwise. What if everything fell into place and he could truly come home again, to Lancaster County, and finally belong? What if he could be part of a family— He cut off the thought. Wishing could lead to dangerous emotions. It didn't end well to long for what you couldn't have. He had learned that the hard way.

When Abby's cries woke John up later that morning, he could tell that he hadn't been asleep long. His body ached and his eyes felt like sandpaper. The sun wasn't up yet, but the sky was tinged pink and yellow with the dawn. Goats bleated in the distance and voices murmured from the farmyard. It must be time for the milking.

He rubbed his eyes, reached down and picked up Abby. "Shhhh, I've got you now, *liebling*." He managed to keep her quiet while he dressed and splashed water on his face from the basin. Then he padded out of the room, down the quiet hallway and into the kitchen to make Abby her morning bottle of formula. The room was still dark, and he lit the propane lamp before he put the water onto the woodstove to heat. He kept Abby cradled in one arm as he went through the motions, then carried her to one of the rocking chairs on the enclosed back porch to feed her the bottle.

He was used to getting up early for his construction job, but he had never sat and savored the gentle beauty of early morning, as the world was waking up. The world felt quiet and new as soft mist floated above the fields. As the sun rose, the light sparkled off the silver frost that clung to the grass in the pastureland. Goat bells clanged from the barnyard along with a woman's laughter. John had missed this. He had missed being Amish.

He cut off the thought fast. Being Amish was a lot more than enjoying a quiet moment in the countryside. But without all the modern distractions, he had time to slow down and enjoy his surroundings. Before he moved to Stoneybrook Farm, he would have been scrolling on his cell phone at a time like this.

Another part of being Amish was working hard. He didn't want anyone thinking he wasn't doing his share. So, he stood up as soon as Abby finished her bottle and headed to the barn. Amanda and Naomi were coming out the door as he arrived. They each carried a bucket of frothy white milk. *"Gude mariye,"* they both said as they hurried past him.

"Good morning. Anything I can do to help?"

"It's our morning to cook breakfast," Amanda said. "You can see if Leah and Miriam need help with the rest of the milking. It'll be time to leave for church before we know it. We're always running late."

"You mean Benji and Leah are always running late," Naomi said. The sisters chuckled as they strode away.

John walked into the earthy-smelling barn. The bleating of goats and stamping of hooves filled the still air, warmed from the body heat of the livestock. The soft whirr of a diesel-powered milking machine hummed in the background. Benjamin and Leah sat on upside-down plastic buckets alongside the milking tables, while Miriam stood to the side, wiping down the equipment with soapy water. Each goat munched happily from troughs attached to the tables they were standing on. John's gaze lingered on Leah for a moment longer than he wanted. Her hair was covered with a green work kerchief that matched the hint of green in her brown eyes. A loose strand of light brown hair fell across her cheek. She was humming under her breath. Something about her looked so happy, so peaceful that he wanted to stay in that moment forever. She seemed as if she belonged, and it made him feel warm and right inside.

Then something rammed him in the leg. His attention shot downward as he yelped. A goat glared at him through black, determined eyes.

Everyone looked up from their work to stare at him.

"Careful!" Leah said. "The goats don't know you yet. They'll butt anyone who doesn't belong."

John took a quick step back, away from the goat. "I'm okay," he said as he rubbed his leg. It was throbbing, and he knew there would be a big bruise there soon.

"Don't let her get to Abby," Leah added.

John felt a flare of irritation. Abby was well out of the way. "I won't. I wouldn't put her in danger."

Leah just tightened her lips and turned back to the goat at her milking table.

Abby cooed at the goat that had butted John. "See, she likes the goats," John said.

"*Vell*, they might not like her," Leah said.

"Everyone likes Abby," John said as he winked at his baby. She gurgled in response.

Leah let out a sharp breath. "You know I didn't mean it that way."

"I only know what you say," John said.

"*Oll recht*, you two." Miriam turned from the milking machine, dropped her washrag into a bucket and put her hands on her hips. "That's enough. At least wait until after breakfast to start in on each other. I don't know what's gotten into you, Leah."

"Gotten into *me*?"

"Just try to hurry up instead of bickering," Miriam said. "Or we'll be late to church again." Miriam's eyes moved to John. "What are you doing out here? You ought to be getting ready for the service. Don't forget the deal. You have to live as Amish while you're here."

"Right. I know. That's why I came out here. To see if I could help with the work."

"Not with a baby in your arms," Miriam said. "We do this every day, so we know what to do. You ought to just take Abby back to the house. Breakfast will be ready soon. And check with Emma about borrowing a diaper bag. Like I said, we're not going to be late to church this time."

"We're always late," Benjamin said.

"Not *we*," Miriam said. "You."

Benjamin flashed her a mischievous grin. "Same thing, since we all ride together."

John stood in the middle of the barn for an awkward

moment. "Okay, well, just let me know if you need any help later. I'm here to work." He wanted to be sure he was pulling his weight.

"Taking care of your child is work," Miriam said. "And there isn't anything else you can do on the Sabbath, since you won't be any good at the milking."

"Don't mind Miriam," Benjamin said. "She likes to boss people around. It's not personal."

Miriam shot Benjamin a look. "I'm not bossy. I'm efficient."

"Is that what you call it?" Benjamin turned back to the goat on his milking table. "Huh. *Oll recht.*"

"He doesn't have any experience," Miriam explained. The milking machines whirred softly in the background, and a goat bleated.

John wasn't sure what else to say, so he turned around and headed out the door. As he left, he heard Benjamin say, "I'm not sure whether to be late on purpose, or to make sure we get there before the service starts. I can't decide which one will get you more riled up. I'd like to prove you wrong, Miriam, but then you'd get to church on time."

John wished he could turn back and crack a joke, or tease Miriam the way Benjamin did. But he knew that it wouldn't come across the right way. Or, more accurately, Miriam wouldn't receive it the right way. The Stoltzfuses had welcomed him onto their farm, but not as a part of their family. He would have to keep to himself, like he did with the *Englisch*. Because he wasn't wanted here either.

Leah had not meant to be hard on John. He had come out to the barn to try to help, and she should have encouraged him. But something had thrown her when she looked up and saw him standing in the early morning light, the sunlight highlighting the sharp plane of his jaw, with Abby snuggled in his arms. She looked tiny compared to his big frame. A man who looked as big and tough as John should be rough around the edges. He shouldn't go around holding babies in barns and looking sweet. It could make a woman start thinking things she shouldn't. Like how good it would feel for him to hold her too. And how protective he might be of her.

Leah could not accept these thoughts, so she turned her annoyance on Miriam instead of herself. "Miriam, you didn't need to be so rude to him."

Miriam's eyebrows shot up. "Me? Did you hear yourself?"

"I heard both of you," Benjamin muttered as he switched off the milking machine.

Leah avoided the subject after that. And she avoided John at breakfast. He held Abby with one arm and bounced her while he shoveled sausage biscuits into his mouth with his free hand. She was tempted to have thoughts about what a good father he was, but she didn't let herself go there. She kept her full attention on her plate instead.

Leah could not help but notice John's hesitation after Benjamin hitched up Clyde and brought the buggy around to the front yard. She wondered what he was thinking and feeling as he stared at the horse. "When's the last time you were in a buggy?" Leah asked as she whisked past John to climb onto the bench seat in the back. He sighed and slowly stepped on board behind her as he cradled Abby in one arm, like a football. "The day we left the Amish, when I was twelve years old." The buggy sank beneath his weight as he dropped onto the seat.

Something in his expression tugged at Leah. "That's a long time."

He sighed. "Yeah."

Abby gurgled and wiggled against John's arm. Leah reached for her. "Can I hold her?"

"Sure." John passed her over, then leaned forward and draped his forearms over his thighs, letting his hands dangle. His legs were too long for the space and the buggy felt crowded, even though it was just the two of them and John had left a big gap between them. Leah studied the wistful expression on his face for a moment before she remembered to look away.

Amanda and Naomi clambered on board. "Hey, scoot over," Amanda said to John. "You're taking up all the space." She was smiling and John smiled back. "Can't help it."

"*Nee*, the *Englisch* must have fed you well, ain't so?"

"Yep." John moved his attention to Leah and his smile faded. Leah knew that the only place for him to go was nearer to her. She felt awkward and slid as close to the far end of the bench seat as she could. John glanced at her, as if asking permission, before he scooted closer. "You okay?" he asked. "Got enough room still?"

Leah swallowed hard. She was more than okay. The feel of him beside her, just grazing the skin of her arm, sent a dash of excitement through her. He smelled like leather and scented soap. She couldn't place the fragrance, except that it was masculine. "I'll manage," she said in what she hoped was a detached tone. It felt like her voice faltered, but she was sure that was her imagination. It was ridiculous for her to be so affected by this man. She was not affected by men. She had more self-control than that. And more dignity.

John was silent during the ride. But Leah was acutely aware of his presence right beside her. Every time Benjamin drove over a bump or a pothole, the buggy lurched and made her bounce against John. His arms and shoulders were as hard as the leather bench seat. Once, when they hit a big ditch in the dirt road and the buggy jolted her, John reached over to steady her. "You all right?" he asked. He made eye contact, and she saw the concern in his soft brown eyes.

She turned away fast and busied her hands by straightening Abby's blanket. "I'm fine." The buggy kept rolling along as Clyde's hooves beat a steady rhythm against the hard-packed earth. Soon they turned onto a paved road and the ride was easier. Leah told herself that it was better this way. But she was keenly aware of the empty space between her and John, now that she wasn't jolting into him.

It felt like the longest ride ever to reach the Kauffman farm, which lay on the outskirts of the Bluebird Hills church district. They passed a farmhouse with wreaths and red ribbons adorning every window. Wooden reindeer grazed in the front yard, their backs dusted with snow. When they cut through downtown Bluebird Hills, each storefront was strung with white lights, and the old-fashioned wrought iron lampposts lining the sidewalk were wrapped in greenery. The sound of Christmas carols drifted down Main Street from hidden speakers. A majestic pine tree strung with lights and silver balls towered over a corner bakery and bookstore.

When the buggy finally rumbled up the dirt driveway and into the farmyard, Leah could sense John tense beside her. She glanced at him and saw the anxiety behind his eyes, even though he seemed to be trying to hide it. He gave her a nod and a strained smile. "Well, we're here."

"Ya." Leah felt like that had been the wrong thing to say, but didn't know what would have been better. She felt like she should tell him that everything would be okay, that everyone would welcome him back and that she would stay by his side even if they didn't. But she couldn't, of course. They weren't friends. She wasn't sure what they were.

John stayed on the bench seat while Amanda and Naomi scooted to the door and dropped onto the ground. The buggy's weight shifted as Benjamin, Emma and Miriam all climbed down from the front seat. A few voices shouted hellos from across the farmyard. Leah followed her sisters, then turned back after her feet hit the hard-packed earth. "You coming?"

"Yeah. Of course." John made his way to the door slowly, like a lumbering bear that didn't want to leave his den.

"I'll give you Abby back," Leah said. "So you have someone with you."

John stared at her for a few beats. *"Danki,"* he said softly. "I mean, thank you. I, uh, appreciate that you thought about that."

Leah waited for him to step down, then passed Abby into his arms. "There're a lot of strangers here for you to meet, ain't so?"

"Yeah." John kept his eyes on Abby instead of looking at the crowd that was hurrying toward them. "It isn't easy coming back, you know."

Leah felt a stab of remorse at how hard she had been on him. "*Nee.* I can only imagine." She hesitated, then stepped closer. "I'll walk in with you. I mean, if you want me to. I don't—"

"Yes. I would appreciate that." Some of the tension behind his eyes softened. "Thanks."

"Anytime."

John's eyes flicked up. The crowd was closing in. He took their last moment of privacy to lean into her and whisper, "I'm not sure what's gotten into you, but I like it."

Leah could feel heat rush into her cheeks as John pulled back and put on an expressionless mask to face the people marching toward him.

John wished that he could be anywhere except in that farmyard, clutching his baby girl while a crowd of strangers closed in on them. He felt transported back to the church services from his childhood, when the Little Creek district began to ostracize his family for his parents' refusal to follow the rules. The women here wore the same range of colorful cape dresses in shades of purple, pink, green and blue. The men had on the same black broadfall trousers, black coats and best-for-Sunday black felt hats. Even the backdrop was achingly familiar. An old white farmhouse with a tin roof and wide porch stood in the distance with a *dawdi haus* beside it. The structure looked like a smaller version of the farmhouse with its tin roof, neatly trimmed hedges, and a simple evergreen wreath hanging on the whitewashed walls. John could feel a tug at his heart and realized he would want to be here, if it weren't for the hard, unyielding faces watching him.

Please help me to face them, he prayed silently. *Don't let me be brought to shame.* John looked up to see Bishop Amos break into a jog to beat the crowd. He was the first to reach them. *"Gude mariye!"* Amos shouted as he sputtered to a stop. The crinkle beside his eyes showed that his smile was genuine. "I want to be sure you know how *willkumm* you are."

John nodded. "Thanks." His eyes shifted beyond the bishop. There were some smiling faces, but most looked solemn. John hoped they were just curious, but he knew better than that.

Amos turned to face his parishioners. "Let's all *willkumm* John Mast, *ya*? He grew up in the Little Creek district, and we're happy to have him back, ain't so?"

Based on the expressions of the people behind Amos, most of them already knew John's story. Word would have spread fast on the Amish telegraph. A prodigal son returning with a secret *Englisch* baby was certainly cause for gossip. He wondered if they knew that he had not really returned. Not in his heart. Not yet, anyway.

A thought flashed through John's mind. In a few weeks from now, on a Sunday morning, he could be lounging on a couch, cuddling Abby while watching television and eating a microwaved breakfast. That *Englisch* life was supposed to be more complicated than this Plain one, but at the moment, it seemed a lot simpler. There would not be any prying eyes or whispers if he took Abby to Ohio. He would make enough to afford day care for her and a decent future for them both. He could live in quiet solitude, with no one to remind him that he was an outcast.

Leah eased closer. "Don't pay attention to the woman coming toward us," she whispered. "She won't have anything *gut* to say."

Leah's words jerked John back to the present. In his daydream, he would have solitude, but he wouldn't have any support. He wouldn't have any family or friends. Not that Leah was a friend. The thought made him feel strange and uncomfortable. But he couldn't ignore the fact that it felt good for her to stand by his side when he felt the most vulnerable.

An elderly woman with a perfectly starched *kapp* and apron strode up to John. Her petite frame and frown lines made her appear frail, but she moved with the energy and efficiency of someone much younger. "I'm Lovina Zook," she said as she peered up at John. Even though she was tiny compared to him, the look on her face showed that she held the higher ground, in her mind at least. The rest of the crowd stood behind her, watching and waiting. John had never felt so exposed. His skin prickled and his face felt hot.

"Hello, Lovina," Leah said in a guarded voice.

Lovina did not look at Leah as she murmured a quick hello in response. Her attention stayed firmly on John. "So, you've been running around with the *Englisch* all these years, ain't so?"

"Uh, I wouldn't put it quite that way..."

"*Vell*, then how would you put it?"

John shook his head and glanced at Leah.

"His parents left," Leah said. "He didn't have a choice."

Lovina grunted. "He does now. Will you be taking the kneeling vows today, young man?"

"Get baptized? Today?" John flinched. "No."

Murmurs moved through the group of people behind Lovina.

"I didn't think so." She clucked her tongue and moved her eyes to Abby. "I hoped you would, for the sake of the *boppli*. But *youngies* like you won't—"

"Mamm!" A young woman pushed her way through the crowd. She was skinny, wore big round glasses, and her brown hair was perfectly in place beneath her *kapp*. She

looked nearly as prim and proper as her mother. "That's enough."

Lovina's lips tightened. "I'm just saying what needs to be said."

"And so am I," the young woman said. She looked to be in her early twenties. "Hi, John. I'm Eliza."

John nodded.

"It's nice to meet you," Eliza said. "We're glad you're here." She looked at her mother with a pointed expression. "Aren't we, *Mamm*?"

Lovina grunted.

"We know you didn't leave by choice. You were just a *kinner*. But what you do now is your choice. We hope you choose to take the kneeling vows and stay with us. We'd *willkumm* you for certain sure."

John shifted his weight from one foot to the other. Eliza had taken up for him, but she wasn't holding back either. "But only if I get baptized."

Eliza stared at him for a moment. The lenses of her big round glasses magnified her eyes as she blinked. "You know as well as I do that you can never truly be one of us unless you're baptized. It's just the way it is."

Leah sighed. "And you always tell it like it is, don't you, Eliza."

Eliza pushed her glasses up her nose with a long, narrow finger. "Of course. Anything else would be dishonest. And it wouldn't do John any *gut*. He deserves to know the truth. There's a reason we live the way we do. We believe it's for the best."

"He's *willkumm* at our house, whether or not he gets baptized," Leah said.

"And Gabriel and I would *willkumm* him at our house too. But he will never belong here as long as he stays *Eng-*

lisch in his heart. And he would never be able to marry one of us either. It's just the way it is. You know the sacrifices it takes to be Amish as well as I do, Leah."

Leah sighed again.

"It's okay, Leah," John said. "She's only being honest."

A good-looking young man with a cheerful expression and a happy glint in his eyes bounded over to them. "I heard my name."

"This is my husband, Gabriel King," Eliza said.

"My *frau* is right. You're *willkumm* at our house anytime. You and the *boppli*."

"Thanks."

Gabriel glanced around and leaned in to John. "I almost left the Amish." He kept his voice low, but Lovina was close enough to hear and her lips tightened into a thin line. "*Vell*, I did leave actually, but I only lasted a few days. It wasn't what I thought it would be. But I do understand wanting to jump the fence."

John wanted to hear more, but Viola Esch appeared in the doorway of the farmhouse and rapped her cane against the porch floorboards to get the crowd's attention, then waved the crowd inside. "You all too busy to make it to the service?" She shot Lovina a look, and Lovina shot her one right back.

Leah chuckled under her breath. "Saved by Viola."

"For now," John whispered. "They'll be at it again as soon as the service ends. And I'm sure we'll have to stay for lunch."

Leah looked at him. She hesitated, then said, "I'll stay with you as much as I can."

The promise meant more to John than he could say. He felt soft inside, like his heart had suddenly gone squishy. Leah Stoltzfus should not make him feel that way. And yet, here he was, wishing he could hold her hand as they walked side by side toward the farmhouse.

Hold her hand? He would never do a thing like that, of course. Just the thought of it was going too far. She was being kind, that was all. He was just desperate for comfort, for an act of kindness that made him feel as if he belonged. As soon as they got back to Stoneybrook Farm, he was sure their squabbling would continue. Maybe he shouldn't even accept her kindness. It might not be a good idea to lower his guard.

But he couldn't resist. And, he couldn't resist thinking about her throughout the three-hour service. The men and women sat on separate sides of the living room on long portable benches, so he was able to sneak quick glances of her. She looked so content as she sang the slow, lilting hymns from the *Ausbund*, or as she listened intently to Bishop Amos preach. Could he find that contentment too? With the Amish? With her?

Not with her. How had that thought slipped into his mind?

When Abby began to fuss, the bishop's wife, Edna, appeared at his side and whisked the baby away so that John could stay for the rest of the service. His body was beginning to ache from sitting on the hard, backless bench, but he wasn't sorry that he had to stay. The familiar German words flowed into him and filled him with a quiet assurance that all was right in the world. Growing up, there had been raised voices and chaos at home, but his time at church had always been predictable and safe. He could count on the same hymns being sung, the same Bible verses being read, the same peanut butter church spread being served after the last sermon ended. There would be no raised voices, no conflict. Sitting there, in the still room, watching snow fall outside the windows and smelling the scent of wood smoke from the fire, he felt at home for the first time in as long as he could remember.

But then, as he shifted his gaze to Leah, he noticed Lovina staring at him through sharp eyes. And she wasn't the only one. This might feel like home, but it wasn't. And he wasn't sure it ever could be, as much as the memories fought inside him to claim otherwise.

Chapter Seven

Leah tried to stay close to John after the service, but she had to help with the kitchen work while the men ate their meal. The women and children would have their turn next. She did manage to get a quick word in as John came through the serving line.

"I know how much you like this," she said as she slid a big slice of homemade bread with peanut butter church spread onto his plate.

His face lit up. "You remembered."

"*Vell*, you did eat an awful lot of it that first night at our house."

He grinned. "Get used to it," he said.

Leah wondered what he meant by that. Was he thinking of staying? Of joining the church? Or was he just joking about his big appetite? She glanced to the side, then back at him and lowered her voice. "How are you holding up?"

John's smile faded. "The service was good. But, uh…" His eyes cut to the crowd beyond them.

"*Ya*. I understand."

John gave her a steady look that made her feel as if he were peeling back layers of her to see inside. "Do you?"

"I don't know." Leah shrugged as she adjusted a serving spoon that rested on the edge of a platter. "Maybe. I don't exactly fit in either." Leah had heard too many times from well-meaning people at church that it was time she settled down with a good man. She was worn-out from avoiding what everyone insisted was inevitable for an Amish woman.

John smiled again, but this time the expression looked wistful instead of joyful. "You sure seem to fit in just fine."

"Then maybe you don't know me well enough." Leah gave a coy smile. Even as she did so, she couldn't believe she had said those words with *that* smile. Was she…flirting? With *John*? She did not flirt. And she certainly did not flirt with *Englisch* men. She knew how dangerous that could be.

"Then maybe you should let me get to know you better."

Leah's heart flip-flopped into her throat. John was flirting back. Except his expression was too serious. It looked like he meant it.

"Ach, vell..." She looked down. "You, uh, want some sauerkraut?"

"I know there's more to you than you've shown me."

Leah's eyes flicked back up to him. "What do you mean?"

"I don't think you're as cold as you pretend to be."

"I'm not cold. I only—"

"Hey, the line's backing up," the man behind John said.

"Right. Sorry." John nodded at Leah, then moved along.

She went back to serving food, but the funny feeling in her would not go back to normal.

Leah lost sight of John for a while. Then, when she finally got a chance to sit down and eat, he was still at a table with the men. She was relieved to see that Gabriel was next to him. But there were also some men at the table who would not be as welcoming. Leah hoped that they weren't being too standoffish. But based on the way they were looking down their noses at John, she suspected it was not going well, despite Gabriel's support.

The farmhouse was filled with the familiar noises of a church Sunday. Babies cried in the next room, and silverware clanged alongside the low murmur of voices from the makeshift tables. Children shouted from the yard, where they played in the snow, bundled in their black winter coats and cloaks. The front door opened, then slammed shut, and a cold blast of air swept in with a child whose cheeks were rosy from the cold.

Leah wondered how soon she could get over to John, without looking too obvious. Then she froze. What was she thinking? Why should she care? She lowered her fork and frowned. Because he was a brother in need, that's all. Well, not quite a brother. An ex-brother, who could be a brother again. Who she hoped would be again, for the sake of his baby. And maybe, if she listened to the catch in her chest, for another reason too.

Did she want him to stay because she wanted him in her life?

Leah shoved a big bite of fruitcake into her mouth and chewed aggressively. Her thoughts had been going to ridiculous places today. She just needed a good night's sleep, that's all. Caleb's crying had kept her awake last night. That's why she wasn't thinking straight.

"You're quiet today," Eliza said. "You've barely spoken the entire meal." Eliza pushed her empty plate away and raised an eyebrow at Leah. "Is it because you're hoping John will join the church?"

"*Ach, vell*, we're all hoping that, ain't so?"

"*Ya*, but you might be hoping for different reasons."

"What reasons?" Sadie Kauffman asked. She and Gabriel's aunt Mary Hochstetler sat opposite Leah and Eliza.

"I think we all know the answer to that," Eliza said.

Sadie shook her head. "Eliza, you're too bold." She tried to hide a smile, but couldn't.

"I'm just—"

"Telling the truth," Leah finished for Eliza as she rolled her eyes.

Eliza frowned. "*Vell*, I am."

"We shouldn't assume anything," Mary said in her gentle, shy way. "Let Leah tell us how she feels."

"Eliza's wrong," Leah said quickly. "I don't feel anything,"

Eliza pointed her fork at Leah. "You're not telling the truth."

"That *is* the truth!" Leah said.

"We all have feelings, whether or not we admit it," Eliza said. "You're feeling *something*."

"Fine. I feel irritated that you're talking about this."

Eliza pushed up her glasses and stared at Leah. "*Vell*, I don't know why. I was just pointing out the obvious."

Leah's eyes cut to the crowd beyond them. "I'm not… You don't think everyone thinks…" Leah groaned. This could turn into a messy situation very quickly. "Look, there is absolutely nothing going on between John and me. And if anyone thinks that…" She had put a lot of effort into convincing people that she didn't want to court anyone, so that the church busybodies would leave her alone. That hadn't always worked, but it would be even worse if they saw a crack in her armor. They would all find a way to meddle, and they wouldn't believe her protests anymore.

"I doubt people are thinking that," Eliza said. "Not yet, anyway. You've made it clear that you won't walk out with anyone."

"Then why did you bring it up?" Leah asked.

"You stood by his side this morning," Eliza said.

"I admire you for that," Sadie cut in. "It couldn't have been easy, with so many people giving him those judgmental looks."

"This is a *gut* church district," Mary said. "Most folks aren't judgmental like that."

"But some are, and that's enough," Sadie said. "No church district is perfect, even *gut* ones like ours."

Mary looked down at her plate. "I'm afraid you're right."

"So," Sadie continued. "I think everyone noticed that you stayed by his side when you arrived."

"I was just being a *gut* friend."

"Some might say that's Benjamin's job, not yours," Eliza said. "There have been a few whispers about it."

"Since this morning?" Leah set down her fork a little too hard, and it clanged against her plate. "That was fast."

Sadie reached over and put her hand on Leah's arm. "It doesn't mean you've done anything wrong."

"Or that you've done anything at all," Mary said. "People will always find something to talk about, whether there's something there or not."

"Ya," Eliza said. "Especially about an ex-Amish *Englischer* who returns with a secret baby."

"It doesn't happen every day," Sadie said.

"That's for certain sure," Eliza said.

"People have been pushing me to find a match and settle down," Leah said. "Now, if they think John and I are sweet on each other, it will really cause a stir."

The three other women stared at Leah intently. "Well, are you?" Eliza asked.

"Nee!"

"Then you have nothing to worry about," Eliza said.

Leah wished it were that simple. For Eliza, everything was always black-and-white. Leah thought that the world had shades of gray. She wished that she could live in Eliza's black-and-white world. It seemed easier that way. More straightforward.

Mary smiled and patted Leah's hand. "How is it going with the *boppli*? Is she doing *oll recht*?"

"*Ya*, she's perfect," Leah said. "Although it is nice that Edna has been taking care of her today. It's *gut* to get a break."

"John seems like a really *gut daed*," Mary said. "I've never seen an Amish *daed* hold his *boppli* as much as John does."

Leah nodded. "He is. You know, not everything the *Englisch* do is bad. A lot of their fathers are more involved than ours are." Leah realized that she was defending John, and worse, the *Englisch*, but she could not seem to stop herself. Something strange was happening inside of her. "I think John learned that while he was out in the world. He saw fathers taking care of their children same as the mothers do. He's never hesitated to change a diaper or stay up with Abby while she cries."

The women were quiet for a moment while they thought about that.

"I don't like to admit that the *Englisch* do anything better than us," Mary said quietly. "It doesn't seem right."

"I think it's okay to recognize that none of us can do

everything right," Leah said. "We all have our strengths and weaknesses."

Leah's eyes shifted to John. He was slouched over his plate with a frown on his face. She wished that she could go offer him a word of encouragement. Perhaps even put a hand on his shoulder. Was that too risky? It could be. Just because John was a good father didn't mean that he would be a faithful friend.

Sadie and Mary left to check on their children, and Eliza slipped away to start clearing dishes. But Leah was too distracted by her thoughts to follow. She picked at the remains of her fruitcake until she was interrupted by a hand on her elbow. She glanced up to see Lovina staring down with her usual stern expression. Leah's chest tightened. She knew from the look on Lovina's face that she had nothing good to say.

"I've been meaning to talk to you," Lovina said.

Leah saw Eliza clearing a table across the room and sighed. She would have gone toe-to-toe with her mother. Maybe that was why Lovina had waited to pounce. Now Leah was cornered and alone. "*Ach, vell*, I wish I had time, but I need to help in the kitchen."

"*Ya*, we both do," Lovina said. "But you can answer my question first."

Leah glanced around in hopes that Benjamin or one of her sisters might appear. But no one noticed her. The men were chatting and sipping strong black coffee beside the fire while the women bustled around, clearing up. Leah sighed. "What question?"

"Why are you taking that business class?"

"I've already been over this with the bishop and the elders. They gave me permission."

"That isn't the answer to my question."

Leah wanted to tell Lovina that she wasn't an elder or a bishop, so it wasn't her business. But the truth was, in Bluebird Hills, everything ended up being Lovina's business, somehow. But unlike Viola, she didn't usually solve problems. She magnified them. "I want to help Miriam. You know how much she's had to shoulder since our parents died."

"Ya." Lovina nodded.

"So if I can learn how to manage the farm better, it would take some of the burden off her. We could be more productive, more efficient, increase our profits." Leah knew this spiel by heart. She was always ready with an answer that would cover the real reason she was avoiding a courtship.

"Mmm. It seems to me that it would honor your parents' memory better if you kept our Amish ways."

"I am keeping our ways. As you know, I have permission."

Lovina's eyes narrowed as she stared at Leah. "And what about the fact that you aren't stepping out with any young men? Have you let anyone drive you home from church or youth group?"

Leah let out a long breath. *"Nee."*

"You're twenty-one years old."

"*Ya*. I'm aware of that."

"It's time for you to marry and have *kinner*. But instead, you're running around taking classes." She paused for effect. "Don't you *want* kinner?"

"Uh, *ya*. I do. Just not now. Not yet."

Lovina's eyes narrowed even more. "Then why wait?"

"Because I want to do other things first. I have dreams of my own."

"You shouldn't have any dreams beyond being a *gut* Amish wife."

"I don't think those two things are mutually exclusive."

"Just listen to you with your fancy *Englisch* talk! 'Mutually exclusive!'" Lovina clucked her tongue. "There's a reason we stop schooling after the eighth grade. You don't need to fill your head with *ideas*."

"I'm just learning accounting and bookkeeping! I'm not getting a degree or going off to school. It's just one online class. For our business. It's allowed, same as using computers and internet for work."

Lovina shook her head. "A big fall often starts from a small stumble."

"This isn't a stumble," a deep voice said from behind Leah. She spun around to see John hovering over her. She wondered how much he had heard.

Lovina's attention jerked from Leah to John. "She's going to school past eighth grade. But I don't expect you to understand."

"I understand what's right and what's wrong." John looked down at her with his steady, brown eyes. "And, anyway, by your own rules you ought to do what the bishop says, right?"

"Right, but—"

"I don't think there's a but. How can a *gut* Amish person like you go against what the church leaders say?"

"Now, wait a minute, young man. I am not going against my bishop."

John raised his eyebrows. "You sure about that?"

Lovina's mouth clamped shut and she pursed her lips. She glared at John for a moment before shaking her head and stalking away.

"You okay?" John asked as soon as Lovina was out of earshot.

"I am now. You stood up for me, and to Lovina Zook of all people. *Danki*."

John smiled. "She doesn't scare me."

"*Vell*, maybe she should."

They both laughed. Then Leah glanced around and lowered her voice. "Seriously, it meant a lot to me."

Their eyes met for a moment, and Leah felt a jolt of connection pass between them. She wanted to move closer to him. She wanted to tell him how she really felt.

But how did she really feel? She wasn't sure anymore. She swallowed hard, hoping that John would say something to help her understand what was happening inside her heart.

But instead, he looked away and murmured, "It was nothing."

"*Nee*, it was something."

It looked like he was considering how to respond. Then he shrugged and said, "You took up for me earlier today, didn't you? It was only right for me to return the favor."

Leah sensed that he was putting distance between them. Was it because his act of kindness had been nothing more than the return of a favor? Maybe the connection that had flared between them had, in reality, been one-sided and he was trying to let her down easy. Why would he be interested in her when Steve had discarded her? Ever since that happened, Leah had been sure that there was something wrong with her. She was not worth keeping.

John could not stop thinking about Leah. It had felt so good to rush in and defend her. Her face had lit up with surprise and maybe even joy. It had been a long time since anyone had looked at him like that—as if he were some kind of hero. Seeing her expression had taken away the sting of the rejection that he had felt all day. If she appreciated him, that rejection from the congregation didn't matter so much.

Stop. John squeezed his eyes shut. He could not think this way. Falling for Leah was a bad idea. He had heard what she had told Lovina about wanting to stay free and independent. He would never interfere with her dreams. She deserved to find fulfillment, and he should not stand in the way.

But, that evening, when he saw her leading the goats down from the turnip patch used for winter foraging, he could not resist going to her. He needed to understand what was happening. Abby was already asleep in her bassinet and Amanda was nearby to keep an eye on her, so it was easy for John to slip away. His feet began taking him up the hillside without his permission. At the same time, his brain told him to be reasonable. He ought to push away this warm feeling inside. Not only was it not what Leah wanted, it wasn't what *he* wanted. He could not risk being trapped here. If he fell in love, there would be no going back. He would have to be baptized and raise his daughter as Amish.

Maybe that was for the best.

No. The cold, aloof looks from the people at church that morning had said it all. How could he ever expect to fit in here? Sure, the congregation was supposed to welcome people back into the fold without holding the past against them. But the way things were supposed to be was not always the way things actually were.

John looked up the hillside to see Leah's form silhouetted by the setting sun. She strode through the pastureland with confidence as the goats ambled alongside, their bells echoing down the hill and into the valley below. The border collies, Chocolate and Chip, circled the goats and urged them onward. In the distance, Ollie barked at an animal beyond the tree line. John wished he felt as confident as Leah looked. He admired her ability to know her own mind, to understand what she wanted and who she was.

He picked his way up the hillside to meet her. The morning's snow had melted in the afternoon sun, but now the puddles were refreezing and he slipped on an icy patch of mud. He didn't know the land like Leah did and had to slow down. Above him, the wide sweep of sky was fading from blue to dark purple and the first stars were winking awake. He heard the soft gurgle of water before he saw the creek that cut through the pastureland. When he reached it, he could make out the glassy shine of water running over stones in the fading light.

"You have to cross here," Leah shouted to him.

John looked up. Chocolate and Chip were herding the goats over a narrow footbridge a few yards away. Their bells clanged and their hooves rattled over the wooden boards. A couple of nannys bleated and hung back until Chip gave a warning bark.

John headed toward Leah and waited for the goats to clear the bridge.

"What are you doing up here?" Leah asked from across the creek before she turned back to the goats. "Go on now," she murmured to a black and white nanny who had stopped to forage on a weed.

"I, uh…" John realized how silly he had been. Why had he barged up here to meet her? What had he been thinking? "I just needed a walk, I guess."

"In the dark?"

"It's not dark yet. Not quite."

Leah looked up from the goats, back to him. "In the goat pasture?"

John shrugged. "I guess so." He waited in silence as the goats trotted over the little wooden bridge. The scene reminded him of the children's story he had heard after he left the Amish. "The Billy Goats Gruff," or something like that. He couldn't quite remember. But he did remember that it involved goats on a bridge. He had liked the story when he was a child. "It's nice out here," he said.

"*Ya.* This is my favorite time of day." Leah gave a contented sigh as her eyes moved past the goats to the sweeping view beyond. "Turn around."

John turned toward the direction from which he had come. The hill sloped downward, creating a dramatic vista of rolling fields and distant farms. Christmas lights twinkled from faraway windows. The Stoltzfus house stood three-quarters of the way down the hill, and below that, in the distant valley, the Yoder pond caught the last glow of sunlight, sparkling in the growing darkness. "It's so peaceful," John murmured.

"*Ya.* I like bringing in the goats. I should have gotten them down sooner, but the sunset was so beautiful this evening that I took my time." Leah smiled. "We'll see what Miriam has to say about that."

John smiled back. "I can tell you love this farm."

"I do." She nodded toward the creek between them. "Did you know that it gets the name Stoneybrook from this creek?"

"No. I didn't know the creek was here."

"Most people don't. It's pretty small, but it's nice to have."

"I've always loved the sound of running water," John said.

"Me too."

John looked back at the pond in the distance. The water was no longer sparkling. The light had faded to a faint, silver glow. Peace hung in the air, along with the quiet rustling of goats moving through the grass as shadows descended on the pastureland. "I can see why you'd take business classes to help keep this place running."

Leah's expression changed. "You overheard me today, when I was talking to Lovina?"

"Some of it."

Leah followed the last goat across the footbridge. "Do you think it's wrong of me?"

"Wrong? No. Why would I think that?"

"Because Amish women are supposed to plan for marriage, not for running a business."

"Okay, but what do *you* want for your life?" John asked softly.

Leah stared at him for a moment. She kept walking, but because she wasn't watching where she was going, she bumped into a goat and stumbled. She caught herself before John could reach her, because the goats blocked his way. Leah laughed. "I'm *oll recht*. I got distracted because no one has ever asked me what I want before. It's very *Englisch* of you."

John frowned. "So you think it's bad I asked?"

"Nee." Leah's eyes looked wistful. "I think it's *wunderbar*."

"Oh." John was so surprised he didn't know what else to say. Leah moved through the goats, patting them on the head or scratching them behind the ears, until she reached him. "So, what do you want?" he repeated.

"I don't know," she said.

John studied the desire in her eyes as she looked out over the pastureland, to where the sun had disappeared behind the darkened hills. The distant Christmas lights looked brighter as the daylight faded. "I think you do," he said softly.

Leah kept staring at the remnants of the sunset for another few beats, then turned away and stretched, as if shaking off sleep. "I just want a chance to experience life, I guess. Help with the farm. Maybe travel a little. Just down to Pinecraft, or wherever the bishop allows." He caught her eye, and she looked down.

"Look me in the eye and tell me that."

"Why?"

"Why not?" John gave a playful smile to soften the serious tone in his voice.

"*Ach*, I don't want to." Leah's brows knitted together as she turned to a goat and patted its neck.

"You don't want to or you can't?"

Leah didn't answer.

"Here's what I think." John stepped closer and patted the goat too. His hand brushed against Leah's, and she glanced up quickly, then down again. Something behind her eyes seemed so vulnerable, so needy and hurt that he wanted to scoop her up and hold her until all that hurt was soothed away. "I think there's something you're not telling me."

"I'm not a liar, John." Her face hardened.

"I don't think you're lying. I just don't think that you're telling the whole truth."

Leah kept running her fingers through the goat's soft winter coat.

"I get wanting to be young and free," John said when she didn't speak. "That's something the *Englisch* value. But something about the way you explain it doesn't sound genuine."

Leah's gaze shot up to John. Her expression was guarded. "No one else has ever questioned me about it. They just tell me I need to get married."

John shrugged. "I guess it's time someone asked about you, then."

Leah shook her head. "It doesn't matter."

"Of course it does."

"I just don't want to get married, okay." The words came out forcefully, with an edge of anger.

John flinched. "Got it. I didn't mean to pry."

"But you did."

"Right. Sorry." He stepped away from the goat and rubbed the back of his neck. "I shouldn't have said anything."

"Let's get to the barn before it gets any darker." Leah began to walk downhill, alongside the goats and clanging bells. John had to pick his way down the hillside quickly, but carefully, to keep up with her. More ice was forming in the puddles of melted snow as the temperature dropped. His eyes and cheeks stung from the cold air. Leah did not speak. John could sense the emotions rippling off of her. He thought it was anger but could not be sure.

Suddenly, she stopped short and spun around. "You wouldn't understand."

John frowned. "Try me."

Leah snorted. "You didn't stay with Abby's *mamm*. You're the type of man to walk away from a woman, ain't so?"

John didn't know how to respond to that. There was so much he wanted to say that he didn't know where to begin. "It wasn't like that," he managed. But the words sounded weak. "I know that seems like a lame excuse." John rubbed his hand across his mouth, then glanced at Leah.

"It does."

"Right." John exhaled. "I uh… Well, we agreed that we didn't want anything more. I told you that my time with her was a mistake. She didn't want a commitment and neither did I. It seemed like a good idea at the time. I know better now. You can't get involved like that and just walk away. There's always a consequence. Some are bigger than others." He glanced over at Leah, but couldn't catch her eyes. She was looking ahead, toward the farmyard. "But I think God can redeem them all."

Leah's head whipped toward him. "It doesn't sound like you were living for *Gott* then, ain't so? But you sure talk like you do now. Which is it?"

John adjusted his black felt hat. "I wasn't living for Him then, but I am now. I'm trying to, anyway." John turned to Leah. He could make out the whites of her eyes in the growing darkness. He was close enough to hear her breathing and smell the scent of pine and earth that clung to her. "There's something about you, Leah."

Leah smiled, but her eyes were sad. "I've heard that before."

John studied her expression. "What do you mean?"

"Nothing. I didn't mean anything. It's just an expression."

John wasn't sure he believed that, but he didn't want to push her. He had already done that too much this conversation. He gave her a little smile. "Well, if you've heard it before, then it must be true. There *is* something about you."

Leah inhaled. Their eyes stayed locked on one another. He stepped closer to her. His mind shouted at him to stay back, to keep his distance emotionally and physically. She had said that she did not want to get married to anyone, ever. And John did not want to get involved with anyone unless the relationship had that potential. He was finished with casual dating. And yet, he could not force himself to back away. His heart pounded inside his chest as he gazed down at her. The rising moon cast a silver glow across her features. She looked beautiful in a plain, honest way. He wanted to hold her hand and tell her that he was falling for her. He wanted to kiss her.

She stared up at him, unblinking eyes fixed on his.

"I don't want any conflict between us," John said. He waited a few beats. A goat bleated nearby, and the tall grass rustled in the breeze. He swallowed hard. "I want us to be friends." It was not the full truth. He wanted something more than friendship. He wanted all the commitment that came with a deeper relationship.

Leah's breath rasped in and out, too quickly. "I... I want that too." Something in her eyes changed. Then, she raised up on her tiptoes and John knew he could not resist the invitation. She wanted him to kiss her. "We can't do this," Leah whispered, even as she eased closer. "I can't let myself..."

John stopped short. Everything in him wanted to pull her close, to breathe her in and tell her that he wanted to plan a future together with her. But he could not do that. She just said that they shouldn't. He had to respect her boundaries. She had doubts about forming a relationship. If he truly cared about her, he would respect her wishes and back away. So he did.

John nodded as he stepped back. "Yeah." He didn't know what else to say, but felt like he should try. "You're right," he added. "This isn't the plan." He wanted her to see that he respected her, that he was trying to understand, even though he didn't know all of her motivations.

Leah did not respond. She just nodded in return, then looked away across the dark pastureland. He studied the outline of her profile. Her jaw looked hard, her face tight. He wished that she would respond. He wished that she would say that she had changed her mind, that she wanted to plan a future with him.

Instead, she walked away and did not look back.

Chapter Eight

Leah refused to cry. She would not allow emotion to take over. Even though her fears had proven true. John was not different. He had no interest in a future with her. She clenched her jaw and strode down the hill with her eyes fixed on the farmhouse. If she focused hard enough then maybe she could keep the tears from forming.

She would not be a part of John's plans. Well, of course she wouldn't be. She had known that from the moment she had laid eyes on him. No, she had known that from the time Steve had shown her how easily a promise could be broken. And John was no different than Steve. Sure, John was making an effort for his child, but that had nothing to do with Leah. She had to remember John's track record when it came to women. He had walked away from Abby's mother. Of course he would not commit to Leah either. Whatever relationship she formed with him would just be something temporary and fun for him. It could never be serious.

Leah shook her head at the surge of longing sweeping through her. No. She would not give in to that longing. If they had kissed, it would have meant nothing to him. Clearly, he was still envisioning a life in the *Englisch* world. A life without her. And she had been foolish to let any thought of a future together slip into her mind. It had just felt so magical—the setting sun, the warmth in his eyes, the way he really saw her, when no one else did. He had known that she was not telling the whole truth about her refusal to marry. He had understood her.

But that didn't matter. Not when his plans were for something other than her. She had fallen to a moment of weakness, that was all. There was nothing between them. Leah pushed away the pain that fluttered just beneath her breastbone, like a bird caught in a trap. She had to gain control over her emotions. She would not allow herself to develop deeper feelings for him. She would not. And she would push away the feelings that had already formed. She reminded herself that he was an outsider, with different values and dreams. Nothing between them could work, even if he were trustworthy. Which he was not.

Leah knew the best thing was to avoid John as much as possible. It was the only way she could stay strong enough to harden her heart to him. The next three days passed slowly. Leah went about the motions of her days, but her thoughts kept pulling back to him, as if drawn by a magnet. She could not concentrate on her business class. She was irritable at the milking and distracted while baking. She forgot to add baking powder to the sugar cookies and had to whip up a new batch while trying to keep Abby from crying.

The pain beneath Leah's breastbone sharpened whenever she watched John with Abby. During lunch, he always held his baby while he ate. Sometimes, when she was fussy, he got up and paced the kitchen floor with her. One of the Stoltzfus sisters would always offer to take her, but John would just shake his head and smile. "She won't be this little for long," he would say. "I want to hold her while I can. Got to get back to work soon."

During those moments, Leah was tempted to believe that John could be faithful, that he could be capable of commitment. But it didn't matter because he did not want to commit to *her*. Would he have kissed her on the hillside, then walked away without a care, if she had not said something to stop them? He would have. She could not let herself forget that. She had to stay strong and accept reality. Just because she wanted John to be different didn't mean he was.

On Wednesday afternoon, Emma and Benjamin asked Leah for advice on a new candy cane scented soap recipe for Christmas sales. Benjamin and Emma had a successful side business selling goat milk soap at the local farmers market and to tourists who stopped by the farm. But Leah could not focus enough to form an opinion. She usually loved anything that made her feel like Christmas, but she couldn't get into the spirit this year. Somehow, the world felt less bright, less dynamic. Less promising. It wasn't fair. She refused to have feelings for any man, ever. And yet here she was, pining away over one against her will.

"Leah." Benjamin's voice pulled Leah out of her thoughts. "Pay attention. Do you like that one? We're also working on a Fresh Cut Christmas Tree scent. Which one do you think would be better?"

Leah sighed and set the sample bar of soap onto the rough wooden work table. "I don't know. They both seem nice, I guess." She stood up and walked out of the tack room, across the barn and into the cold sunlight. She pulled her black cloak together as the air cut through her cotton cape dress. Leah heard Benjamin's footsteps behind her and turned around. "Don't say a word about it."

He grinned. "You don't know what I'm going to say."

Leah pinched the bridge of her nose and squeezed her eyes shut. "Look, I know you have a way of picking up on what's going on with me because we're twins, but there's no need to bring it up."

"Hate to say this, but it doesn't take a twin to see what's going on. You're being pretty obvious."

Leah opened her eyes and dropped her hand. "How obvious? Do you think John knows?"

"Knows what?"

Leah scowled at her brother. "You said you already knew."

"*Vell*, I know you're avoiding him and acting funny whenever you run into him. What happened?"

"Nothing happened. I'm fine. Everything's fine. Unless John thinks that I'm avoiding him. Then I'm not fine."

"Of course he's noticed. Miriam brought it up last night while you were up in the high pasture."

Leah's stomach dropped. "She brought it up to John?"

"*Nee*. Just to us. She wanted our opinion on it."

"Why?"

"To know if it's time for him to move on. He isn't *wilkumme* here if it isn't *gut* for you."

Leah puffed up her cheeks, then let out the air. If John left, that would solve the problem, wouldn't it? Her heart shouted otherwise. "Just leave it be. I'm fine. Everything's fine. I'm not kicking him out."

John chuckled. "*Nee,* but Miriam might."

"She wouldn't."

"Only if you need her to."

"I don't." Leah crossed her arms and looked away.

Benjamin waited a few beats, then softened his tone. "So what happened?"

Leah shook her head. "Nothing happened. That's the problem."

"Oh. Okay. I get it." Benjamin waited for Leah to say more. But instead, she just looked past the fence to the old oak tree. The leaves had fallen and the bare branches were silhouetted against the blue sky.

"Maybe it's for the best," Benjamin said after a moment. "He might not commit to the faith."

"Of course it's for the best!" Leah had not meant to shout the words. She glanced around to see if anyone had noticed. Only Belinda. The goose's head shot up, and she stared at Leah with glassy black eyes, then flapped her wings and waddled away.

"You don't sound like you believe that," Benjamin said.

"Of course I do." Leah's tone was as sharp as her expression.

Benjamin put up his hands, palms out. "*Oll recht*, it's for the best. Got it."

"Look, I have to study. I've got a big exam coming up and I'm going to fail it. That's what really matters." She marched away before Benjamin could say anything else.

Leah liked to study on the enclosed porch in the wintertime, where she could enjoy the view and hear the quiet hum of the farmyard while she worked. She carried an old blanket, a stack of books and a mug of hot apple cider to one of the rocking chairs and settled in. The room was chilly, and the hot mug felt good in her hands. She wrapped the blanket around her, tucked in her feet and opened her book.

Goats bleated in the distance, wind rustled the evergreen garland hung from the porch railing, and Belinda's webbed feet slapped the ground as she waddled from one end of her territory to another, keeping a sharp eye out for intruders. From the side of the farmhouse came the occasional grinding of a saw or the thud of a hammer. Leah tried to ignore those sounds.

She reread a few passages in her textbook, but found her eyes wandering to the sweeping view of the pastures that sloped upward. She noticed a tall pine tree standing alone, and imagined how she would decorate it for Christmas with shiny red balls and colorful lights, if she were *Englisch*. Leah blamed John for the thought and forced her eyes back to the page, straightened her back and read the passage again. She closed her eyes and tried to repeat the information that she had just read out loud. She couldn't remember half of it. The frustration of the last three days bubbled over, and she flung the textbook as hard as she could. It flew through the air, end over end, and landed with a heavy thump on the worn wooden floorboards at the other end of the enclosed porch.

"You missed."

Leah's attention shot to the side. John was standing in the doorway, wearing a leather work belt full of tools.

"If I was aiming for you, I certain sure would have hit you."

John chuckled. "I bet so." His gaze shifted to where the book lay on the floor. "Everything *oll recht*?"

"*Ya*. Of course."

"Just tossing textbooks for fun, huh?"

Leah frowned. "I've got a big exam on Friday and I haven't studied enough. It's too late now." It was a lot more than that, of course. But it was easy to fall back on her usual excuse, even though she wanted to shout that the real problem was that she could not trust him. She would never tell him, of course. Then he would know that she cared. That would make the rejection even more humiliating.

"It's never too late." John jogged over to the textbook, picked it up and trotted back to Leah. "Okay," he said as he dropped into the rocking chair beside her. "Where do we start?" He passed her the textbook.

"Danki." Leah opened the book and began flipping through the pages. She stopped and looked over at him. He was leaning back in the chair with his head resting against the wall and his long legs stretched out. He took up a lot of space. Too much. Especially in her heart. "Why do you care?" she asked.

"Because you should have what you want in life."

John's words unsettled her. No one besides Benjamin had ever said anything like that to her before. Most people just told her to hurry up and get married. They never asked what *she* wanted.

The trouble was, she *did* want to get married. She wanted a lifetime of moments like this one. She wanted to feel seen and heard. She wanted to sit side by side with a man she could talk to, a man she could trust. Leah had to remind herself that John was not that man. That man did not exist.

"It's okay," John said. "I'm not asking you out to dinner. I just want to help you with this."

"I didn't think—"

"I know. But you look like you've seen a ghost."

"What? *Nee*, I'm fine."

John's playful expression shifted to something more serious. He looked into her eyes. "I wish I knew what you're thinking."

So many thoughts flashed through Leah's mind. There was so much that she wanted to say. But instead, she tapped the open page of the textbook with her finger. "I'm thinking that I need to pass this test."

Leah thought John's face fell, for just a moment, before he hid it with a smile, although she could not be sure. "Right," he said. "Hand over the book and I'll call it out to you, okay?"

"*Ya*. Sounds *gut*."

Time passed quickly as they studied together. The interaction felt easy and natural, once Leah told herself that it meant nothing and she let her guard down. But then, Leah caught John watching her with an expression that she could not read. The crinkle in his brow looked like concern, but perhaps he was just tired. Or curious. She did not know and she refused to ask him. She could not risk believing the things he might tell her.

After the sun had moved toward the horizon and Leah was able to recite everything she needed to know, John closed the book with a quiet thump. "This was nice," he said as he looked at her with that steady, disarming gaze of his.

Leah looked away quickly. It had begun to snow. She watched the white snowflakes settle on the bright red berries of the holly bush that grew beside the porch.

"You don't think so?" John asked quietly.

"I'm just surprised to hear you say it, because you have other plans, remember?"

John let out a heavy exhale. "Right." He shifted his weight on the blanket. "I'm not the only one."

Leah twisted in her chair to turn toward him. "Are you going to stay Amish or are you going back to the *Englisch*?"

"I guess that depends."

"On what?"

"I don't know. A lot of things."

"Like what?"

"How welcome I feel here." He scratched his jaw. "How much I can fit in."

"You don't feel welcome?"

His eyes softened. "When I'm around you I do. After the way you stood by me at the service, I mean." He gave her a little teasing smile. "Maybe not before then." That serious expression returned. "But now..."

"Oh." Leah could not pull her gaze away. Her heart beat in her ears as she stared into his deep brown eyes. The words froze in her mouth.

"I think I could stay." He swallowed hard. "I think I want to stay." He paused, and time felt suspended. The entire world stopped. Then he took a deep, steadying breath, as if gathering his courage. "If you want me to. Because you would be the reason."

Leah felt her world spinning away from her. This could change everything.

And she did not know if she could fight it anymore.

That night, John was still reeling from his conversation with Leah. What had he been thinking? Why had he said those things to her?

Because he meant them.

The realization sent a warm wave through him. If he stayed here, he could face people like Lovina, as long as he had Leah by his side. In fact, the entire Stoltzfus family would probably stand with him. Not to mention Bishop Amos, Edna and Viola. And more too, probably. Yes, there would always be folks who did not approve of him, who would never let him forget his past. But maybe that wouldn't be so bad, if he knew that there were also plenty of people who wanted him here, in Bluebird Hills. Maybe he could finally come home.

John's pulse quickened at the thought. He could imagine a life at Stoneybrook Farm. Abby would grow up surrounded by people who loved her. She would roam the rolling hills and pastureland, swim in the Yoders' pond, learn to tend the goats and bake the shoofly pies that he had grown up on.

Stop. He was getting ahead of himself. He had not been invited to stay long-term. But, after the way Leah looked at him during their conversation on the enclosed porch, he could believe it might all work out. Could their dreams and needs merge together to become one? Yes, of course they could. They would fit together, just right, to fill in the spaces the other one needed. He would never find a woman who understood him and supported him like Leah among the *Englisch*. More than that, he would never find a woman like Leah. Period. She was a perfect blend of everything he admired in a person. Self-reliant, determined, confident, capable, intelligent, faithful.

Had they been at each other's throats just a few days ago? It seemed impossible. It was time he was honest with himself. They had squabbled because they had been drawn to one another. And they both knew that attraction was dangerous, because their hearts were in two different worlds that clashed with each other.

But what if he stayed? What if he accepted her world? *His* world.

John glanced down at Abby. She was sleeping peacefully in her bassinet. Now was a good time to slip out to the barn and check his cell phone. Maybe it was time to let that company in Ohio know that he wasn't interested in the job. At the very least, he ought to check and see if they had contacted him. He realized that it would be a relief if they had reached out to tell him the position was no longer available. Then he wouldn't have to make the decision himself.

Suddenly, he had to know.

John adjusted Abby's blanket. If she woke up in the brief time that he was gone, one of the Stoltzfus sisters would hear and come to check that everything was okay. He picked up the kerosene lamp from the crate beside his bed and padded out of the room. The hallway was empty and quiet. He pulled on his work boots, then shut the front door softly, so the noise didn't wake anyone. The farmyard lay still beneath the moonlight as he crossed to the goat barn. Snow crunched beneath his boots. Far away, where the gravel driveway met the highway, he could see the twinkle of *Englisch* Christmas lights.

John's stomach churned as he pushed open the door and strode across the concrete floor. A few goats scrambled up from where they lay in the straw and bleated as he passed them. John didn't slow down. He could not get to his phone fast enough. He needed to know if his *Englisch* job was still an option. His emotions warred within him as he imagined the different paths his life could take from here.

The kerosene lantern cast strange shadows against the wooden walls as he entered the tack room. The shadows moved as he did, then shrunk as he reached the corner of the room. He tore open the flaps of his cardboard box and pulled out his phone. It felt familiar to hold it again, to have the whole world, accessible right there, in his hand. But did it feel right?

He did not know.

John pressed the on button and waited as the phone came to life. His jaw ached from the tension. As soon as the screen lit up, he touched the phone icon. No messages.

He scanned the recent calls list. Nothing. John let out his breath. He had not realized that he had been holding it.

Did he really wish that the job had left him a message telling him they had filled the position? Yes and no. He would no longer have the future that he had planned and worked for over the last decade. It was scary to think of that door shutting. But it was also exhilarating to think of staying. To not have anything tempting him away.

"What are you doing?" Leah's voice asked from behind him.

John spun around. "What are *you* doing?"

"We have a sick goat. I came out to check on her. But that's not the point. You're the one who needs to answer the question. You said you wanted to stay and now—"

"I said I think I want to stay," John interrupted.

Leah shook her head. "Regardless, you promised to live as Amish while you're here. Why are you on your phone?"

"I'm not breaking the *Ordnung*."

"Of course you are. Phones are only allowed for business."

"That's why I'm using it."

"Then why are you sneaking around to do it? You don't need to hide it if it's allowed."

John hesitated.

"You *are* hiding something." Leah raised her kerosene lantern so that his features fell into the light. "I can see it on your face."

John let out a long breath. "I'm sorry. I'm not sneaking around, and I'm not breaking the *Ordnung*. But maybe I didn't tell you everything about my plans."

"What do you mean?" Leah's hand began to tremble, shaking the kerosene lantern and making the shadows quiver against the wooden walls.

John told himself it was not a big deal. It was just a job

offer. People got them all the time. So why had he kept it to himself? He should have said something earlier, because now the disappointment in Leah's eyes was more than he could bear. But he had made no promises. He had been careful to keep his distance.

But they had formed a connection anyway.

Or he had, at least. He could not tell with her. She was like a closed door, her thoughts and hopes locked away inside. He rubbed his mouth and looked away. "I, uh, have a job offer from a big construction company in Ohio. It's a *gut* job. A *gut* opportunity. For me and for Abby."

Leah took a step back. "I knew it..."

"I'm sorry, Leah, I never meant to—"

"You've been planning to leave this entire time. You didn't even consider staying, did you?" She shook her head. "I almost let my guard down and believed you. I even thought that you might take the kneeling vows." She took another step back. "The whole time, you knew you were leaving. You were already planning to go that night when we brought the goats in together. Or on the porch, when we studied together—none of it meant anything to you."

"No!" John put up his hand. "I promise. You've got it all wrong."

"*Nee*. I've got it right. I just wanted to believe that you were different, even though I knew better." The expression on her face nearly broke John's heart. He wanted so badly to put his arms around her and hold her close. But he did not, of course.

"So it meant something to you?" John said the words softly, while his heart pounded inside his chest. He knew it was a risk to ask that question. But he had to know. Had she been falling for him too? Had she been pushing him away on purpose?

Leah hesitated, as if trying to decide how to respond. Something flickered out behind her eyes and her expression hardened. "I know how *Englischers* are. It's always a game to you."

"A game? No. Never."

"Then what was it?"

John froze. He did not know how to answer that. Was he ready to accept his feelings for Leah and fully commit to the Amish way of life? Was it fair to her to make that leap if he wasn't 100 percent sure? He had feelings for her. He did know that. But were they enough? And could he be the Amish partner she deserved? The seconds ticked by as John tried to find the words without knowing the right answers. He could hear the sharp hiss of Leah's breath. Her chest rose and fell too quickly.

John hesitated a moment too long. Leah spun around and marched across the tack room, her kerosene lantern swinging hard and casting wild, moving shadows across the walls. She stopped when she reached the doorway, but did not turn around. "You should leave," she said quietly. Then she slammed the door shut behind her.

He stared at the space where she had stood a moment ago. He should have said something. But what could he have said? He never should have considered staying here for good. Leah held something against him, and he did not know what it was. Maybe it was simply that he was afraid to commit to her and to the Amish. Or maybe it was something more that she was not willing to say. Either way, this was not where he belonged, especially now that he had a good opportunity among the *Englisch*.

He would just have to force down the feelings in his heart that shouted otherwise.

Chapter Nine

Leah marched into the kitchen the next morning with a tight jaw and eyes that flashed with emotion. Miriam stood at the stove as grease crackled and popped on a skillet, and Benjamin was halfway inside the refrigerator, reaching for a bottle of milk. Thankfully, John was not there. "Where is everyone?" Leah asked.

"By everyone, do you mean John?" Benjamin asked in a playful tone. But as soon as he straightened up and saw Leah, his expression and tone changed. "What's wrong?" He did not take his eyes off of her as he closed the refrigerator door.

"It's John," Leah said in a low voice, just in case he was near.

Miriam turned around from the skillet quickly, the spatula still in her hand. "What happened?"

They both stared at her. The room was so silent that she could hear the hum of the propane motor that powered the refrigerator. "He never planned on staying. He's got a job lined up in Ohio with the *Englisch*."

Miriam clicked off the burner, set down the spatula and nodded at Leah. "Go on."

"That's all."

Miriam and Benjamin exchanged a quick glance.

"Hey, what's the matter with all of you?" Naomi asked as she strode into the kitchen with Amanda close on her heels. "Did the goats get out again or something?"

"John's going back to the *Englisch*," Leah said.

Emma walked into the kitchen with Caleb in her arms. "What? When?" She glanced around the room. "Why am I always the last to hear about anything?"

"You're not," Amanda said. "We don't know what's going on either."

Emma's face fell when she looked at Leah. "You know, don't you, Leah?"

"I caught him on his cell phone late last night."

"Wait." Miriam's brows came together, and Leah recognized the look right away. "Why were you with him in the middle of the night?"

"Stop it, Miriam. You don't have to treat me like I'm a child and you're my *mamm*."

"*Vell*, apparently I do."

"Give her a chance to explain, Miriam," Benjamin said.

"I ran into him in the barn."

"When you went out to give the second dose of medication to the goats," Miriam said, but her eyes were still guarded.

"Ya." Leah made an exaggerated motion with her arms. "And there he was, on his phone!"

"Maybe there was a *gut* reason," Emma said. Benjamin pulled out a chair for her, then took the baby from her arms. "That's possible, isn't it?" Emma asked as she sat down.

"He never planned to stay," Leah said.

"He said that?" Amanda asked.

"He didn't have to," Leah said.

"I thought he was settling in here," Naomi said. "He seemed to get on pretty well at the service."

"Lovina and some of the others gave him a hard time," Benjamin pointed out as he readjusted Caleb against his shoulder. "He might not feel *willkumme*."

"*I* made him feel *willkumme*!" Leah said. She realized too late that she had shouted the words.

An awkward silence fell across the room. "Not really," Miriam said after a moment. "It seemed like you wanted him gone from the moment he arrived here."

"*Vell*, maybe at first, but then everything..." Leah looked away and frowned. How could she possibly explain it?

"Everything what?" Amanda asked.

"Everything changed," Leah said.

Naomi raised her eyebrows. Miriam let out a quick, sharp breath. Emma looked down at the table.

"Go on," Leah said. "Somebody say something."

"I don't think it's a *gut* idea to leave your heart unguarded around an *Englisch* man," Miriam said quietly.

"I know that!" Leah wanted to pick up a plate and throw it across the room. She clenched her fists instead. "Don't you think I know that?"

Leah glared at Miriam, but she couldn't bear the expression on her sister's face. It was something between sadness and sympathy. Leah looked away. "Nothing happened and nothing will. He was never serious. About anything."

"I thought he was serious about coming back," Miriam said. "I know he was conflicted. But I thought he wanted to try." She turned back to the counter and gazed out the window, to where the sun was rising above the tree line at the bottom of the hill. "I shouldn't have invited him into our home."

"Let's hear what he has to say," Benjamin said.

"I don't understand." Amanda turned to Leah. "Have you and John been stepping out together without us knowing?"

"*Nee*, of course not."

"She just wanted to," Miriam said. "I should have protected her from this."

"Stop it, Miriam. I never said I wanted to step out with him."

"You didn't have to."

"I'm fine. I'm not even upset."

"Now *you* stop it, Leah," Naomi said.

Miriam clucked her tongue, and Benjamin sighed.

Footsteps padded down the hallway, then paused before they reached the doorway.

"John!" Miriam shouted. "We need to talk."

There was a heavy sigh from the hallway before John walked through the open door. All faces turned to him. Benjamin's expression was gentle, Amanda's and Naomi's were fierce, while Miriam's was guarded. Emma was still sitting at the table, fidgeting with the edge of a crocheted place mat, refusing to look up. Leah stood alone with her hands on her hips, eyes flashing.

"You sure you want me in here?" John asked. His voice sounded resigned. He was holding Abby as she slept soundly in his arms.

Leah caught the sadness behind his eyes and faltered for a moment. She reminded herself to be strong. "I told them that you're leaving."

"I never—"

"Don't you realize that it's best to raise Abby Amish?" Amanda interrupted before John could finish his sentence.

"She's a part of this family now," Emma said softly.

"How can you think of taking her away?" Naomi asked.

"Now, hold on." John took a step forward. "You're not being fair about this."

"*We're* not being fair?" Miriam shook her head slowly. "You could have told us your plans. You could have been honest with us. You shouldn't have let us get attached to Abby if you knew you weren't going to stay. You shouldn't have let..." Miriam pushed her sleeves up, then shook her head again. "You shouldn't have led Leah on."

"I never..." John closed his eyes, took a deep breath and let it out again.

"I didn't say you did that," Leah said. She wanted to sink into the floor. "John, I never said anything about us." Now she had made it worse. "Because there is no us. There was never an *us*. They have it all wrong."

"Leah, let me handle this," Miriam said.

"*Nee*, not when you say things like that. This isn't about you."

"It's about all of us, because all of us love Abby. And all of us trusted John to be honest about his intentions."

"Okay, fine. But don't bring John and *me* into it."

Miriam stared at Leah for a moment without responding.

"Stop looking at me like that," Leah said. "I know that look. You think you know better than I do."

"I think I'm just more willing to speak the truth."

Leah's eyes cut to John, then back to Miriam. "Can we please wait to have this conversation until he's not in the room," she said through gritted teeth.

Miriam shook her head. "He needs to account for his actions."

John sighed. He looked older than he had the day before. "For what actions? Taking you up on your offer? I never made any promises."

"Not saying something is the same as a lie," Amanda said.

"We don't know that," Benjamin said. "Let him explain."

"Look, I don't have to explain anything." John rubbed Abby's back in slow circles. "You were kind to help my baby and me. But it was a mistake to take you up on the offer to live here. I'm sorry. I don't owe you anything. And I never asked for any of this."

"We thought you would *kumme* back to the Amish if we gave you the chance," Amanda said.

"You should have told us that you weren't going to try," Leah said. Her jaw ached from clenching her teeth.

"I did try," John said. He let out a long, slow breath of air. "But I can see that my first instinct was right. I was never really welcome here." His eyes cut to Leah. "None of you sees me as one of you."

And then he turned around and walked out of the room.

Leah's heart fell to the floorboards as she watched him go. How had this happened?

More to the point, what *had* happened? All she knew was that she wanted to run after him, fling herself into his arms and tell him to never leave. She did no such thing, of course. She stood rooted to the kitchen floor, listening to her pulse pound in her ears, wishing she had never met John Mast.

John's head was throbbing with hurt and outrage. The entire family had condemned him, just as he had feared they would. This was why he had been so reluctant to stay.

And now, they had proven him right. He would never be accepted here. He would never belong.

His first instinct was to get out of there as fast as he could. He made it to the driveway before he realized that he had no way to leave. His car was across the county, with his ex-coworker. He didn't own a horse and buggy. He would have to call a driver. He stormed across the farmyard with Abby cradled against his shoulder, scattering the chickens in his path. They clucked, flapped their wings and ran away as he neared them. As soon as he passed, they bent their heads back to the ground and pecked the earth again.

John made it to the door of the barn before he began to see reason. He should not leave, even if he had the transportation. Not yet, anyway. His emotions had run high, and now that his blood was no longer beating in his ears, he was able to think a little more clearly. He had made a commitment and he would keep it. He would not be like his parents, who had run off when they felt too much pressure. He would stay and finish the addition on the house. Then he would leave.

The thought of leaving felt wrong, deep inside. But what else could he do? Now he knew that the entire Stoltzfus family looked at him as an outsider. They were so quick to judge that they had not even given him a chance to explain himself. Only Benjamin had tried to get John's side of the story, but his sisters had shouted him down.

Abby shifted in his arms and murmured in her sleep. John stopped and patted her back. What exactly had happened in the kitchen? He could not quite remember. It had all played out so fast. He had felt so hurt and defensive that the memory was blurred. But he was sure that Leah and the Stoltzfus family did not understand. That much he did remember clearly.

He skipped breakfast and brought the bassinet outside so Abby could sleep in the sun while he worked. He would not ask anyone to watch her. The temperature that day was mild for December, so she would be warm enough in her fleece baby bunting, with the portable kerosene heater keeping her extra snug. If the weather turned, he would take her under the big tarps he had set up to protect his work. John's jaw clenched and unclenched as he measured a length of lumber. He would not ask anyone for anything anymore. He had been independent before he came here and he would go back to being that way. He had not needed anyone for the last decade and he did not need anyone now.

Except for Abby. He glanced over at her. The hood of her baby bunting had ears sewn on, so she looked like a little bear cub. She was so sweet, so perfect. He would take her to Ohio, where he could support her. Just the two of them. He swallowed hard. If he told himself enough times that he still wanted that, he could almost believe it.

John had not been working long when Leah strode around the corner, then stopped short.

"You're still here."

"Where else would I be?"

Leah stared at him. Her mouth opened, then closed. Tears welled in her eyes, and she wiped them away quickly, then turned away and began to march back in the direction she had come.

"Wait."

Leah stopped, but did not turn around.

"Please," John said as gently as he could. He sighed and set the measuring tape on the sawhorse.

"I thought you'd left." She was still facing the other direction. Her arms were rigid by her sides, her hands balled into fists.

"Not yet. I said I'd finish the job, so I'll finish the job."

"Right." She turned around to face him. "You're just here to finish the job."

"Don't worry. I won't..." He glanced at Abby, then back at Leah. "We'll be gone by Christmas."

Leah's expression hardened. She nodded. *"Oll recht."* She strode over to Abby and scooped her out of the bassinet. "But she stays with me while you're working. I'm going to be with her as much as I can, while I can." Leah stared down at Abby, forced a smile and kissed the top of her head, then turned and walked away. John could not stop himself from watching them. Leah and Abby looked so natural, so right together.

Leah faltered, then turned back around. She stared right into John's eyes. "Why didn't you tell me you had a job offer?"

"I tried."

"Not very hard. How long have you known about it?"

"Since the day I moved in here."

Leah snorted. "Plenty of time to mention it."

John exhaled. "I meant that I tried to explain it to you last night, in the barn. But you wouldn't give me a chance. And then this morning, you and your sisters jumped on me before I could say a thing. You all think you know me, but you don't." John's chest tightened. He wanted to draw closer to Leah, not pull farther away. But what else could he do? She refused to see him for who he really was, even after he tried to let his guard down and show her. Maybe he hadn't shown her enough. Maybe if he were open and vulnerable, she would understand where he was coming from.

No, he had shown her too much, and now she didn't like what she had seen. Pulling back from her was the only thing that made sense now.

Leah shook her head. "You had plenty of chances before last night. You've been here for nearly a week."

John felt a prickle of guilt. Why had he kept the job a secret? Because he had been afraid that she would react like this. She wasn't being reasonable. None of them were. He felt a prickle of guilt, then pushed it away. Anger flared as he remembered how many people had looked at him with the same expression that Leah wore now. She thought she knew better than him, that he was a lost cause, a black sheep. She had given up on him, same as everyone else. Maybe she never believed in him at all. Hadn't she been the harshest to him when he first arrived? "I didn't tell you because I was afraid that you would react like this," John said before he could stop himself. "And it isn't anyone's business but mine. Why do you care so much, anyway?"

Leah's face crumpled. John thought that she would raise her voice, but instead her response came out softly, almost in a whisper. "Why do I care?" Her lip trembled. "I..." She tightened her mouth, shook her head and strode away without looking back.

Chapter Ten

Leah had almost told John the truth. The need to admit how she felt about him was eating her up inside. But she had stayed strong. She had not admitted that she had fallen for him. She was proud of herself for that. She had learned her lesson from Steve and protected herself this time. She just wished that it didn't hurt as much to push someone away as it did to be pushed away.

Leah and John did not speak for the rest of the day. They only grunted and nodded at one another as they passed Abby back and forth between them. John did not spend much time with the family. He was polite, but only spoke when spoken to. He threw himself into his work, and the sound of his hammer rang across the yard from sunrise to sunset.

On Friday, Abby took her exam. As she hunched over the computer in the office nook of the production building, the blue light casting a glow across the cool, dim interior, Leah wished for John. His calm, laid-back presence had reassured her when they had studied together. He had made her feel like she could succeed. Something about his big, sturdy build and serious brown eyes made her feel safe.

Leah frowned and sat up straighter. Her thoughts were

going to terrible places. An *Englischer* making her feel safe. Ha! John was not interested in keeping the faith. He was not interested in her. She hit the return button on the keyboard to start the test. *Focus, Leah.*

Leah reread the question and clicked the cursor. The next question popped up. Her thoughts veered back to John. He shared the workload. He took care of his baby *and* worked hard labor on the farm. He encouraged her to pursue her dreams. Of course he made her feel safe.

Stop it. Leah pushed John out of her head and clenched her jaw. She would focus. She would not think of him. She would not.

She failed at that, but she did pass the test with flying colors. Partially thanks to John's help.

At breakfast on Saturday morning the atmosphere was strained and silent, as it had been ever since the family had confronted John about the job. The sound of silverware clinking was painfully loud. Outside, Ollie's bark drifted in through the glass windowpane and a plane buzzed overhead. Leah took a sip of milk, swallowed and set the glass onto the dining room table. "I got an A on my final exam. The semester's over, and we're on Christmas break now."

Benjamin raised his glass of milk into the air. "You did it!"

"*Gut* job, Leah," Miriam said. "You're a hard worker."

"So you admit it?"

Miriam rolled her eyes but couldn't hide a slight smile.

Leah glanced at John. His eyes held a spark of joy for the first time since their falling-out. And he was smiling. A real, genuine smile. But as soon as their eyes connected, he looked away. "Congratulations," he said as he shifted his attention to the garland of holly laid across the center of the table. "You deserve it."

There was so much that Leah wanted to say. "Thanks for making it possible," she murmured. It was all she could manage. And even that made her cheeks burn.

John's gazed swung back to her. "I didn't do anything."

"You helped me study."

"You just needed a little encouragement. It was all you. Don't forget that." He stood up abruptly and dropped his napkin onto his plate. "I need to get an early start."

Benjamin let out a low whistle as soon as John was out of earshot. "He sure has fallen for you, Leah."

"Then why isn't he talking to me?"

"Why aren't *you* talking to *him*?"

"You shouldn't encourage them, Benji," Miriam said. "John's heart isn't with the Amish. Leah's doing the right thing to avoid him. Let him finish the job, then leave. Sometimes things don't work out the way we wish they could."

"Look, I know how hard it is to communicate," Benjamin said. "What my brain wants to say never quite comes out of my mouth the right way. Seems like the two of you just aren't saying what you need to say."

Leah snorted. "*Ach*, I think John has said plenty."

"He's had more than enough time to explain himself," Miriam said. "He could walk back in here right now and tell us that he wants to return to the faith. But instead, he's barely talking to us. And he's planning to leave as soon as he finishes the job. That says it all."

Benjamin and Emma exchanged a glance.

"Would you invite John to stay here for good if he wanted to?" Emma asked.

"Sure." Miriam shook her head. "But he's made his choice. He's going to stay *Englisch.* I wish he had given us a chance, but his heart was never in it."

"I'm not so sure about that," Benjamin said.

"Then why is he leaving?" Amanda asked.

Naomi made a stabbing motion in the air with her fork. "Exactly."

"Maybe he doesn't feel *willkumm* here anymore," Benjamin said. "And maybe he doesn't feel like he can tell us that."

Miriam set down the butter knife in her hand. "We're sharing our table with him, our home."

"He's been through a lot. You can't understand what it's like, being an outsider."

Leah knew that Benjamin understood what it felt like to be an outsider more than Miriam. His developmental disability, dyspraxia, had always made him feel different, especially when other people expected him to just overcome it, as if that were possible. It wasn't, of course. "You have a way of understanding people, Benji," Leah said.

Emma leaned closer to Benjamin and put her hand on his arm. "Why don't you talk to John?"

Benjamin laid his hand over Emma's and shook his head. "*Nee*. I'd just get my words mixed up. I wouldn't be able to say what I mean. And anyway, I'm not the right one to do that. It should be Leah."

"Nope." Leah pushed her plate away. She couldn't finish her pancakes. "No way. There's no reason why I should do it. There's nothing between us. Nothing."

Emma and Benjamin exchanged another glance.

"Leah's better off without him," Miriam said. "He's not going to stay Amish."

"He might," Benjamin said.

"You can't change a person just because you want to," Miriam said.

"I'm not talking about changing him." Benjamin leaned forward. "I'm saying that we need to try to understand him."

"What's there to understand?" Miriam pushed her chair back. "We all need to get to work. We're letting an *Englischer* get a head start on us."

Leah wanted to say that she did understand John. He was an *Englisch* man, acting like an *Englisch* man. He was not to be trusted.

Leah threw herself into her work so that she wouldn't have time to think and the day would pass quickly. That afternoon, she was scooping the vitamin mix out of a big plastic bucket to add to the goat feed when Emma strolled into the barn with Caleb in her arms. Leah wiped her forehead and looked up.

"Naomi's watching Abby, and I've got my hands full with Caleb. Can you run over to the Yoders? They're doing the winter pruning on the peach trees today and might need help. You know Amos and Edna aren't as young as they used to be."

Leah straightened up and brushed her hands off on her apron. "Sure. But don't you want to go so you can visit your aunt and uncle?"

"*Ach, nee*, Caleb's been fussy. I'm going to try to put him down for a nap." She nodded toward the door. "You go on and stay for a visit."

Leah wouldn't mind getting away for a few minutes. She had been moping around over John long enough. It was past time to get him out of her mind. A slice of Edna's famous fruitcake might do the trick. At least temporarily. And, if she kept pushing John out of her thoughts long enough, then surely she would get over him eventually.

Leah didn't bother to wash her face or change from her green work kerchief into her *kapp*. Edna would have been working all day too, so she would understand. They visited often enough that there were no formalities between the two families. Leah snapped the lid onto the plastic bucket of vitamin feed and headed outside, into the bright sunlight. She squinted as she made her way across the farmyard. The air was cold and fresh, even though the sun was shining, and Leah was glad that she was wearing her heavy wool stockings along with her cloak.

When Leah reached the fence, Ollie trotted over and gave a low whine. His tail wagged back and forth slowly. "You stay here, *bu*, and watch the goats with Belinda. I'll be back soon." She patted his head before slipping through the gate and latching it behind her. The field that separated Stoneybrook Farm from the Yoder property was wide and open. Leah swung her arms and breathed in the rich scent of pine needles and damp earth as she trotted down the hill. In the valley, the pond had frozen over and sunlight sparkled against the ice. The Yoders' empty sunflower field lay in front of the water, waiting for warmer weather, when it would burst into bloom again. Beside the fallow field, and behind the old farmhouse, lay the peach orchard. The bare trees stood in neat, orderly rows, like soldiers at attention. The scene felt right. It was as familiar as her own home, since she had spent her childhood crossing over the property line to see Amos and Edna, or to play with Emma when she came from Ohio each summer to visit her aunt and uncle. With no children of their own, Amos and Edna had always been eager to welcome *kinner*.

Leah cut down the hill, directly to the farmhouse. She passed the spacious kitchen garden in the side yard, with its wide rows of winter vegetables: beets, cabbages, parsnips, potatoes, shallots, turnips and squash. Behind the garden, a modest wreath made of pine boughs hung on the side of the house. Leah breathed in deeply. She loved the smell of damp earth and fresh-cut pine. She loved the simplicity of a Plain Christmas. She loved home. She could never leave to go *Englisch*. Never.

A sense of loss tugged at her, deep down. She could never have a future with John, even if he wanted one.

Well, that was fine. She didn't want a future with him. She was letting a schoolgirl crush get the best of her. She had felt a connection, but it had been fake. John had been stringing her along. Telling her pretty lies. It had all been a game to him. Although his expression had seemed so earnest this morning, over breakfast. *It was all you*, he had said of her success. And his eyes had looked so painfully honest in that moment.

Leah rounded the corner of the farmhouse to see Viola's buggy parked out front. Bad timing. Somehow, she would already know everything that had happened. And she would definitely have something to say. Leah raised her chin and threw back her shoulders as she trotted up the front porch steps. She had to brace herself for the conversation that was coming. Maybe she should just turn around now, before it was too late.

The front door swung open and Viola appeared in the entranceway before Leah could escape. "Ah! There you are. What took you so long?"

"You were expecting me?"

Viola waved her hand in a vague motion. "Something about coming to help with the winter pruning, ain't so?"

"Ya."

"*Vell, kumme* have some fruitcake first." It was just like Viola to invite someone in, when it wasn't even her house.

Leah followed Viola into the entry hall and let the screen door slam shut behind her.

"Fruitcake, *ya*?" Edna shouted from the kitchen.

"Ya," Leah said, loudly enough for her voice to carry.

Edna bustled out of the kitchen with a plate in each hand. Eliza followed close behind, carrying a tray with mugs of hot tea.

"We've got everything ready," Edna said. "*Kumme* to the living room."

"Danki," Leah said, then turned to Eliza. "Hey, Eliza. I didn't know you were here."

"Just stopping by for a visit."

"Tomorrow's Visiting Sunday."

Eliza's glasses slipped down her nose a fraction, but she couldn't take her hand off the tray to push them up. So she tilted her chin up and peered down her nose at Leah. "Got a head start on the visiting, I guess."

"Don't you work at the gift shop on Saturdays?"

"Hmm. Not today. Gabriel took over for me."

Leah frowned. She was beginning to feel like this was an ambush.

"So many questions!" Viola said as she waved her cane toward the living room. Leah sighed and followed. A black potbellied stove filled the small room with heat and the scent of wood smoke. Edna's quilts lay folded on a quilt rack beside a wicker rocking chair and over the back of the couch. A white candle in a ring of holly sat in the center of the coffee table.

"I'm glad you stopped by," Edna said as she settled into the wicker rocking chair. She passed a slice of fruitcake to Leah.

"*Danki*. I knew I could count on you for my favorite Christmas treat."

"And here's your tea," Eliza said as she set the tray onto the coffee table. "Peppermint." Leah sat on the couch and picked up one of the mugs. Warm steam that smelled like a candy cane rose to meet her.

"And you can help with the winter pruning?" Eliza leaned forward as she waited for the answer.

"*Ya*. That's why Emma sent me over." Leah could tell that Eliza was up to something. They all were.

Eliza nodded. Her eyes cut toward the side yard and, beyond that, Stoneybrook Farm, as she tapped a finger against her mug.

"Stop that, Eliza," Viola said. "You're making me nervous." Viola picked up her fork. "Now, Leah, tell us what's going on with John. We hear that he's going back to the *Englisch*." Viola took a big bite of fruitcake while she waited for the answer.

"*Ach*, nothing's going on. He's been planning on taking a job in Ohio and didn't tell us about it. That's all."

Viola narrowed her eyes and leaned toward Leah. "That's all?"

"Ya."

"You seemed pretty sweet on each other at the Sunday service," Eliza said.

And there it was. Leah set down her fruitcake. She had not touched it yet. "Eliza, we talked about this at lunch after the service, remember? John and I were just being nice to each other."

"Is that what you *youngies* are calling it these days?" Viola asked before popping another bite of cake into her mouth.

"We are just friends. Not even that. We are just acquaintances. Or maybe we *were* friends. But not anymore."

"You don't sound very sure of anything," Viola said.

"I'm sure we're not sweet on each other."

"But you two got along so well at the service," Edna said. She gave Leah an encouraging look.

"We did. I guess."

"So what happened?" Eliza asked. "I hear you two aren't speaking now."

"How did you hear that?"

"Emma told us," Viola said.

"Don't blame her," Edna said. "You know she didn't have a choice. Not when Viola and Eliza were teamed up against her."

"We were not against her," Eliza said. "We're for her. Same as we're for Leah. We just needed to know what was going on, so we can help."

"How can we help when no one tells us what's going on?" Viola asked. She gave Leah a chastising look.

"I'm pretty sure everyone always tells you everything, Viola," Leah muttered.

"You certain sure haven't," Viola said.

"Because there's nothing to tell," Leah said.

"Do you think John might be persuaded to stay?" Edna asked.

"Nee..." Leah shook her head. She could feel the emotion welling up within her. She could not let it out. "And it doesn't matter now."

"Of course it does," Viola said. "We haven't lost him yet."

"You could persuade him to stay," Eliza said. "It would be best for him and for Abby."

"I know it would be. But you've got it all wrong. He's set on leaving. What I say doesn't mean anything to him."

"We think you should try," Edna said. "There's nothing to lose and everything to gain."

There was her pride, for starters. But she knew that

wasn't a good argument. The Amish were supposed to stay humble, no matter what. She voiced her second thought, instead. "Why would he listen to me? We're barely speaking."

"Leah, you're exactly the person he *would* listen to," Eliza said.

"That just isn't true!"

Viola's cane rapped hard against the floor. "Leah. Cut the foolishness. Anyone can see that you are sweet on each other. The only reason that you're not courting is because you're too stubborn. That's why you have to talk to him. Find out what he's thinking. Why is he so set on leaving?"

"It isn't my business."

"Then make it your business," Viola said. "Don't you care about what happens to him and Abby? Do you really want them going back to the *Englisch*?"

"Of course not. I want him to come back to the faith and raise Abby in it. But—"

"Gut." Viola gave a decisive nod. "Then talk to him."

"I think what Viola is trying to say is that—" Edna began.

"I am saying exactly what I want to say," Viola interrupted. "I may be old, but I still know how to talk."

"I just meant..." Edna tried to hide a smile. "Never mind."

"It doesn't matter, anyway," Leah said. "I already told you that he doesn't want to talk to me."

"*Vell*, what do you expect when you won't talk to him?" Viola asked.

"You sound like Miriam now," Leah muttered.

"What Viola means is that John might be trying to give you space, out of respect."

"I said what I meant to say, Edna," Viola said. "Didn't we just go over that?"

"Why would he do that?" Leah asked Edna.

Eliza balanced her plate on her knees and pushed up her glasses. "Because he's a *gut* man who wants to do the right thing?"

"Or he never cared about me as much as I cared about him," Leah said.

"Aha!" Eliza's slim forefinger swung around to point at Leah. "So you *do* care about him."

Leah scowled and shrank back into her chair. "I didn't mean it to come out that way."

Eliza raised an eyebrow. "You meant to lie instead?"

"*Nee*. Of course not. But I won't fall for an *Englischer*." *Or any man*, she added silently. But she knew deep down that she had already failed to keep that promise to herself. She could no longer suppress the emotions that John brought to the surface.

"Which is why you need to talk to him and find out if there is anything you can do to convince him to stay," Eliza said in a matter-of-fact tone. "Then you wouldn't be falling for an *Englischer*."

"I don't want to have to convince him."

The three other women all stared at Leah. She looked away so that she did not have to meet their eyes. Her gaze followed the long gravel driveway that wound down the hill to the highway in the distance. Miniature cars sped along the black ribbon of pavement, the sun flashing against chrome as they zipped past. On the other side of the road, the *Englisch* farm had a wooden crèche in the yard and a white picket fence draped with lights and red ribbon. "I want him to stay because he wants to stay here, with me."

Edna sighed and put a hand on Leah's arm. "So you *do* have feelings for him."

"*Nee*. I refuse."

Edna nodded. "I think I understand now. And he might have feelings for you too, but you won't know if you don't talk to him."

"Did Benji and Emma put you up to this?" Leah asked.

"You're avoiding my question," Edna said gently.

Leah grunted. "Shouldn't he be the one to make the first move?"

"No one's asking you to propose."

"Vell, I should hope not," Leah muttered.

Edna ignored Leah's retort. "Just be willing to start a conversation. Once he leaves, it will be too late. You may regret it for the rest of your life if you don't say something while you still can."

"Better to hurt your pride now, then to hurt your heart for good," Eliza said.

Leah stiffened. She had not thought of it like that before. "This isn't about my pride."

The women exchanged glances.

"Of course it is," Viola said when she looked back at Leah.

"I'm not foolish enough to—" Leah cut herself off. "Never mind."

Edna squeezed Leah's arm. "Maybe it's not all pride. Maybe it's fear too."

Leah frowned. She was not going to admit how right Edna was. Although, she would argue that it wasn't just fear driving her. Some of it was wisdom too. She had learned her lesson the first time. She did not have to learn it again.

Edna's gaze moved beyond Leah, to the side yard, and her expression shifted. "Time to get to pruning, *ya*?"

"I haven't eaten my cake yet."

Viola pushed herself up using her cane. "We'll wrap it for you. Time to get going. It's Saturday, not Visiting Sunday."

Leah looked up at Viola. "Are you trying to get rid of me?"

Viola and Eliza glanced at one another.

"We just have some chores to get done before Christmas, that's all," Edna said. "And it would be a big help if you could finish the pruning for Amos and me. There're just a few trees left."

"Ya," Eliza said. "Chores. Now you go on. And don't forget what we said."

"There're some shears in the garden shed behind the house," Edna said.

Leah stood up slowly. *"Oll recht.* I'll get going." She knew this was going to be some kind of trap, but there was nothing to do but walk right into it. So she headed around to the back of the house, grabbed a pair of sheers and work gloves and strolled into the orchard. The sunlight filtered through the branches to cast dappled light across the frosty ground. A cold breeze swept a swirl of flurries through the air. Leah took a deep, relaxing breath. She loved it here, in the solitary beauty of the peach grove. Everything was ordered and predictable, each tree carefully planted exactly where it should be.

She had grown up helping the Yoders tend these trees, and she knew exactly what to do. She stood beneath a tree, closed her eyes and visualized which branches to trim. She smiled and opened her eyes.

John was standing in the distance, watching her.

"What are you doing here?" Leah asked.

"I could ask you the same thing." When Leah didn't respond, John added, "Emma sent me out here."

"She already sent me."

"Yeah, I can see that."

Leah crossed her arms. "I knew this was a setup."

"Looks like it."

Leah felt a stab of humiliation. What if John thought she was playing matchmaker with him? "I didn't tell them to do this. I'm not in on it."

"I didn't say you were."

"You might have thought it."

He winked at her. "Should I?"

That wink sent a wave of warmth through her and weakened her knees. But Steve had known how to turn playful when it suited him too. This could be a way to manipulate her into letting down her guard. She cleared her throat. "I don't think we should joke around when we're not even talking."

John hesitated. He scratched his jawline. "Why aren't we talking, Leah?" His tone was sad and serious at the same time.

"Because you led me on." There, she had said it and she could not take it back. She hoped Emma and the rest of them were happy now.

"Is that really what you think?" John's voice quivered with emotion. He looked away, and when his eyes met hers again, he had regained his calm demeanor. "I meant everything I said to you."

"What about the things you didn't say?"

John began to walk toward her. His brown eyes stayed on hers, hard and steady, as he strode closer. He stopped when he was a few feet away. Leah had to tilt her face up to meet his eyes. "Can you understand why I didn't tell you about the job?"

"Nee."

"Can you try?"

"Maybe."

"Have you tried to imagine what it's like, coming back to the Amish, after being away for a decade?"

Leah didn't answer. There was a lump in her throat and she was sweating beneath her cape dress, despite the cold. She could feel her heart beating inside her chest. *"Nee."* Leah took one step closer to John. She tilted her face a little more to keep eye contact. "But I want you to tell me."

John swallowed hard. "I've never belonged anywhere. Not with the *Englisch* and not with the Amish. I'm caught between two worlds, and neither one really wants me. I thought… I thought maybe you understood that."

"You never told me."

"I couldn't."

Ollie barked in the distance. Leah shifted her weight. "Maybe I would understand, if you were willing to open up and tell me."

John raised his eyebrows. "I could say the same thing to you."

Leah grunted and looked away. "I'll be fine if you go back to the *Englisch*," she said after a long pause.

"I know. You're independent. You can handle being on your own." He stared at her, and Leah knew that he wanted to say more, but he did not. John had just opened up to her and told her how he really felt. She could sense that there was more he wanted to say. But he would not unless she opened that door a little wider. But she knew if she did, she would not be able to close it again. She would not be able to bear being alone again. She would not be able to wall off her heart after this.

Leah squeezed her hands into fists. She would be the one to say it. She would be brave enough. Her inner alarm went off, warning her that she was about to cross the line and plunge herself into danger. It was reckless. It was foolish. She knew better.

And she had never felt so excited.

John's heart was beating out of his chest. All he wanted was to reach down and scoop Leah into his arms. He wanted to tell her that he had fallen for her. But he would not. He would not pressure her when she had made it clear that she wanted to keep her distance. And besides, how could they make it work? The Stoltzfus family had turned on him. He was not wanted here. Leah would have to give up too much to be with him.

Leah stared up into his eyes. Her brown hair fell out of the green work kerchief in wisps, and she had a smudge of dirt on her chin. She had never looked more beautiful. Her lips parted and time stood still. Everything in John's body shouted to know what she was about to say.

"I don't know how to feel."

"Don't overthink it," John said.

"I can't let myself fall for you."

His chest tightened. "Because I'm *Englisch*? You can't see me any other way?"

"It's more than that." Leah looked down at her hands. She was wearing work gloves that were too big for her. "I fell for an *Englischer* last year. During my *Rumspringa*."

John's eyes widened. He had not expected that.

"I let things go too far. We were in love." Leah breathed in, then out. Her eyes were still on her hands. "Or I thought we were. He left me for a woman from Philadelphia. They're married with a baby, last I heard."

"So he led you on, then abandoned you."

Leah swallowed hard. "*Ya*. That pretty much sums it up."

Everything made sense now. "Leah, I'm so sorry." John wanted so badly to reach out and touch her, but he kept his arms by his sides. She needed her space now. He wanted her to know how much he respected her.

"I guess it doesn't sound like that big a deal. It happens to a lot of women."

"It's still a big deal." John studied her expression. "Big enough that it made you give up on marriage altogether, didn't it?"

Leah nodded without looking up. "I didn't want to tell you. No one knows. I tell everyone that I want other things for my life, that I'm just not interested in settling down. It's too humiliating to admit the truth."

"No. He's the one who should feel humiliated. He's the one who lied."

"I made mistakes..."

"So did I."

Leah looked up. *"Ya."* She managed a small smile. "That's true."

John chuckled. "Now, that's the Leah I know." He hesitated. If there was ever a moment to say the words burning inside, this was it. He said a silent prayer for the courage to take the risk. "That's the Leah I fell for."

Leah inhaled sharply. "You..."

"Yes. I've fallen for you. Completely." Their eyes locked. Time slowed down. All that existed was the two of them, alone in the peach grove, as snow fell softly to dust her kerchief and cloak with delicate white crystals. The world felt still and soft, suspended in a winter wonderland. Anything could happen.

"I... I'm afraid to let myself feel anything for you," Leah whispered.

"I know. That's okay. We don't have to rush anything.

There's time." He could wait a lifetime, if that's what it took for her to heal. She was worth it.

"*Nee*, there's not. What about the job?"

"You mean more to me than the job or what it could do for my life."

"So, you'll stay?"

He wanted to say yes. He could wait on her, but could he wait on her here, among the Amish? It was a huge, lifetime commitment. He was ready to commit to Leah, but to staying in a community that had rejected him? That would not be so easy. "I don't know what to do, Leah. I'm not one of you. Not anymore. And I don't think your family wants me to stay."

Leah's brows furrowed. "Of course they do."

"Remember how quick they were to judge? None of them asked how I felt or what had really happened. They just jumped to conclusions about me."

"They were worried about Abby."

"They should know that I have her best interests in mind. I'm her father."

Leah sighed. "I know. You're right. We all should have been more understanding. I'm sorry. But no matter how they feel, you shouldn't let that interfere with us."

"You're right about that. But it isn't so straightforward. I know how hard it is to be estranged from the people you love, to be torn between different beliefs. I won't do that to you."

A tear formed in Leah's eye and slid down her cheek. "And I won't ask you to stay when it isn't what you really want."

"I want to stay here, with you." John couldn't imagine a life with the *Englisch* now. Not when Leah was here, with the Amish.

Leah wiped her face with the back of her heavy work glove. "*Nee.* You have to stay here because you want to commit to the faith. Not just for me. If you stay for me, it will never work. You'll resent me eventually. You'll never feel like you're one of us. You have to know you belong here."

"I don't know if I will ever feel that way."

They stared at one another. John's heart ached as he studied her clear brown eyes. She had told the truth. But it was a hard truth, one he did not want to hear. He wished love could be like a fairy tale, with an easy, straightforward happily ever after. "I don't know what to do," he admitted.

"I don't either."

Chapter Eleven

John and Leah stood in silence, facing each other. Leah's cheeks were red from the cold, and her eyes sparkled with unshed tears. John did not know how to feel. Opposing emotions fought within him. He was both hopeful and afraid, certain and unsure. He knew that he would do everything he could to be with Leah, but would it be enough to make it work?

"We have to trust *Gott* with our future," Leah said, her eyes on him. "There has to be a way forward."

Before John could answer, a shout echoed down the hillside. His eyes jerked toward Stoneybrook Farm. Naomi was flying down the hill, her *kapp* strings fluttering behind her and her black winter boots throwing up dirt. "John! *Kumme* quick! It's Abby!"

A fear like John had never known surged through him. It made him feel sick and weak inside. "What's happened?" he shouted as he took off toward Naomi.

"She's sick!" Naomi managed to say as she gasped for breath. "Hurry!" She skidded to a stop as John sprinted past her.

John ran faster than he had ever run before. He could hear Leah following behind him but knew she could not keep up. "Go!" Leah shouted, her breath coming hard.

"I'll meet you there!" He flew up the hill, tore through the gate, raced across the farmyard and took the front porch steps two at a time. His heart pounded in his throat and his head pulsed. Abby had to be okay. She had to be. He threw open the front door and burst inside. "Where is she?" he shouted down the empty hallway.

"We're in here," Miriam called out from the living room.

John sprinted down the hall, turned the corner fast and tumbled into the living room. Miriam held Abby in her arms while Emma, Benjamin and Amanda hovered nearby. He heard the front door open, then slam shut, and footsteps pounded down the hallway. Leah and Naomi rushed into the room, breathing hard. Leah hurried to his side while Naomi hovered in the doorway.

There was a hushed solemnity in the room. It was so quiet that John could hear the floorboards squeaking beneath his weight. His breath sounded too loud as it rasped in and out. His heart was still beating fast from running. "What's wrong?" he asked as he reached for Abby, and Miriam gently passed her into his arms. She was sleeping sweetly, wrapped in a soft pink blanket.

"I don't know." Miriam frowned. "She seems to be okay now. But I think something is wrong. I'm so sorry, John."

"What happened?"

"It seemed like she was having trouble breathing," Emma said.

"And her color was wrong," Amanda added as she eased closer to get a better look at Abby. "It's better now."

"She's still too pale," John said. He felt a quiet chill ripple through him. He could sense that something was wrong with his child.

"We've called Elizabeth Troyer from our business phone," Miriam said. "She's on her way."

"The bishop lets us have a phone in the production building for our business," Naomi said.

John nodded. He had noticed the phone and knew that some Amish businesses used telephones. His eyes stayed on Abby. Did she look okay? Was her breathing normal? He wasn't sure. He did not have enough experience with babies. He had never felt so helpless in his life. His strength and height could not help him now. He was powerless to save his child if there was something seriously wrong. He had never felt so small.

"Elizabeth was my midwife," Emma said. "She'll know what to do."

"Ya." Leah said. "Abby will be in good hands."

It felt good to have Leah close. Somehow the fear didn't feel so big with her beside him.

"Elizabeth is Mennonite so she understands our ways," Leah continued. "She looks after most of the expectant mothers and new babies in Bluebird Hills."

It wasn't long before they heard the low rumble of a car engine, then tires crunching against gravel. There was a firm, confident knock on the front door a moment later.

"*Kumme* in!" Benjamin shouted.

The door creaked open, then clicked shut again, followed by rapid footsteps. A stout woman in her fifties appeared in the doorway. She wore a serious, competent expression along with a simple calf-length dress in a delicate floral print. A lacy circle of white fabric was pinned over her bun. The covering was small enough that most of her curly brown hair was visible.

Elizabeth wasted no time. Her attention shot to Abby, and she quickly scooped her from John's arms. "Tell me exactly what happened and when," Elizabeth said as she carried Abby to the couch, then sat down with her. She pulled a stethoscope out of her black leather bag.

Miriam repeated what she had told John.

Elizabeth nodded, then carefully unwrapped the pink blanket and listened to Abby's heartbeat. Abby's eyes opened and she began to cry. "Shhhh," Elizabeth murmured. "It's okay." But her expression said otherwise.

"When was her last well check?"

John's heart sank. "I don't know."

Elizabeth's eyes jerked to John. "You don't know?"

"It's not John's fault," Miriam said. "He didn't know about Abby until a few days ago. We don't know her medical history."

"Ah. I see." Elizabeth studied John for a moment before turning her attention back to Abby. John felt as if she could see right through him, to all his failures.

"I made an appointment for a well check, but it's not until next week," John said.

"So, we have no idea if she's been seen by a doctor before?" Elizabeth cut him off. "We don't have any medical records on her?"

John took off his black felt hat and raked his fingers through his hair. He should know his baby's medical history. But how could he when he did not even know he had baby until last week? "There must be records at the hospital where she was born."

Elizabeth gave a quick nod, then listened to Abby's heart again. The room was so quiet that John could hear Leah breathe beside him. He reached out and took her hand. She looked up at him. "It will be okay," she whispered. "You're not alone in this." John squeezed her hand. Nothing could mean more to him than those words.

Elizabeth removed the stethoscope from her ears and looked up at John. “What about the mother’s medical history? Any heart condition?”

“Heart condition? No, I…” John swallowed hard. Shame washed over him. “I didn’t really know her.”

“Right,” Elizabeth said in a clipped voice. “We need to take Abby in to see a doctor that can run some tests. I don’t like what I’m hearing. And I don’t like the symptoms that you described. And her color is still off.”

“I don’t understand,” John said. “What’s wrong with her? You said it was going to be okay.”

Elizabeth hesitated. “I hope that it will be. But she needs to see a doctor as soon as possible.”

The rest of the day passed in a blur. John still couldn’t believe what was happening when they returned home from the hospital late that night, exhausted and afraid. Abby had a congenital heart condition. She needed surgery.

“It’s my fault,” John said as he cradled Abby in his arms. The baby blanket covered a heart monitor, but they all knew it was there, a reminder of the danger that Abby faced.

“It isn’t your fault,” Leah said. “Don’t say that. Don’t ever think that.”

John sank down onto the couch. The rest of the family had gone to bed. It had been a long day and the milking would come early. The world would not stop just because his baby was sick, even though he felt like it should. He could not accept that the sun would keep rising, that the grass would keep growing, the cars would keep zipping along the highway at the end of the driveway, even if Abby were no longer here.

No. He could not think like that. He could not let himself imagine the worst. John swallowed hard and pressed his face against the crown of Abby's head. She smelled like baby. "I don't know what to do," he whispered.

"Yes, you do," Leah said, her voice fierce. "You're going to keep going. Abby will have the surgery and then everything will be okay."

"We don't know that."

Leah did not answer for a moment. *"Nee,"* she said finally. "We don't. But as Amish, we believe that everything that happens is *Gott*'s will. Let that be a comfort to you."

John raised his head to look at her. Abby stirred in her sleep, snuggled against his chest. "Leah, I'm not Amish."

Leah met his eyes with a sure, steady gaze. "You were and you could be again. You need *Gott* now more than ever."

"I've known *Gott* without being Amish," John said. "I don't have to wear these clothes or go without electricity for that."

"Maybe not, but it gives you a community that will always stand with you in times like this."

"Not all of them stand with me, Leah." While cradling Abby in one arm, he raised a hand to rub his forehead. "We've already been over this. You can't just come back to the Amish and be accepted as one of them. I know it's supposed to work like that, but it doesn't. People don't forget." He lowered his hand to adjust Abby's blanket. "But none of that matters anymore. I have to pay for the surgery. And the doctor said there may be more after this one. That takes a lot of money. Right now, we don't even have health insurance."

Leah's face fell. "What are you saying?"

John sighed. "I don't have a choice anymore. I have

to have a job that will give Abby good health insurance. She's going to need a lot of care."

"Amish don't use health insurance. We take care of our own."

"Yes, if they are part of the community. But I'm not. I just showed back up a few days ago. I'm not even baptized. No one is going to step up to cover these expenses. And even if they wanted to, how could they? This is going to cost thousands of dollars. No one has that kind of money in our church district, even if they all contributed."

They sat in silence for a moment, watching Abby's chest rise and fall.

"So, you're going to take the construction job in Ohio?" Leah asked after a while.

"I don't have a choice anymore."

"What if you did?" Leah asked. "What if there was a way?"

"There isn't. It's best not to wish for what we can't have. I'm sorry, Leah. I can't stay here with you." John's chest felt like it was made of lead. He could not bear breaking her heart. Or his own.

John headed out to the barn first thing the next morning. He had to call East Valley Construction and accept the job. Snow had fallen in the night, and the world was covered in a smooth, white blanket. The chickens were huddled in their coop, and the dogs were inside the barn with the goats, leaving the farmyard still and quiet. The *Englischers* across the highway had left their Christmas lights on, and they twinkled against the overcast sky. Snow crunched beneath John's boots as he trudged past the woodpile and into the barn. The interior was dim, and John had to light the kerosene lantern to see clearly. He remembered how many times he had held a lantern in the dark. The flickering yellow light felt comforting. So did the sounds and smells of a barn full of livestock.

He thought of the table that the Stoltzfus sisters were setting in the dining room right now. There would be home-cooked biscuits and gravy, sausage and egg casserole, strong black coffee and slices of fruitcake for dessert. The plain furnishings and bare walls would feel familiar and safe. So would the smell of wood smoke from the potbellied stove. Best of all would be the laughter and banter of the people around the table. He would miss that most of all.

John stopped. The lantern kept swinging, even though he was standing still, making the shadows on the wall rise and fall. He was thinking of all the things he would miss here. Had he missed anything about the *Englisch* world over the last week? He frowned in concentration. At first, it had been hard to go without his phone. He had had a habit of playing games on it to unwind. But that had faded quickly. Conversation had filled in those empty spaces. And he didn't need a crutch to help him relax here. Not when he could sit in silence, listening to the sounds of nature and taking the time to watch the sunset. No, he did not miss his old life.

John walked slowly to the tack room. Each step felt like he was going further away from what he wanted. Because he was. It wasn't until he knew he had to go that he realized how much he wanted to stay. Of course, he had wanted to stay for Leah. But now, it felt like much more. He wanted to stay and be Amish. He wanted this life. All of it. He had finally found home again.

And now he had to leave.

John sighed as he set down the kerosene lantern and pulled his phone from the cardboard box. He reminded himself that if he stayed, he would not be accepted. Wanting to stay wouldn't change that. Appreciating the Amish way of life wouldn't make him one of them. His parents had considered coming back once, and the cold response they received had made them leave again. He could not go through that again.

John held the phone in his hand, telling himself to press the on button. He had to do this. There was no other choice. He tightened his jaw, held down the button and waited for the phone to power up. Each second felt like an eternity. As soon as the screen lit up, he touched the green phone icon. He needed to get this over with. He scrolled, found the number and touched it. The phone dialed, then rang. He waited.

"Stop!" Leah shouted from the doorway behind him.

John hung up the phone and turned to her. "What's wrong?"

She shook her head. "Don't call them yet."

John didn't think he could go through this again. His heart was still aching from their last conversation. "Leah, I'm sorry, but—"

"Just give me forty-eight hours," Leah interrupted. "Forty-eight hours. That's all I'm asking."

John sighed. He wanted to give her whatever she wanted. But this was only going to prolong the pain.

"Trust me." Leah stepped closer. "If I'm supposed to let myself trust you, then you have to do the same for me."

"I never asked you to trust me."

"*Nee*, but you want me to, ain't so?"

"Yes. Of course I do."

Leah gave a firm nod. "*Oll recht*, then it's settled. You'll wait to call."

John stared at the phone in his hand. In one quick call,

everything would change. He would put himself on a path that would take him away from Leah for good. And away from the faith that he now knew he wanted. He sighed and set down the phone. "Leah, it means a lot to me that you want me to stay and that you'd work hard to try to make it happen." He stepped closer, put a hand on her arm and looked into her eyes. She needed to understand, even though it would hurt. "But you can't solve this. It just isn't possible."

"Maybe not, but I have to try."

John frowned. He couldn't make her see what he saw. "Leah, even if you somehow solve the problem of the medical expenses, there's still the fact that I'm not welcome here."

"Plenty of people support you here. Edna, Amos, Benjamin, me—"

"I know," John interrupted. "And that means something, it really does. But it's not enough if the rest of the district keeps treating me like an outsider. It's worth it to me to stay here to be with you. But you've already told me that wouldn't work unless I want to be here for the faith too. Plus, how can I raise Abby in a place that will penalize her for being my daughter? People in the Little Creek district rejected me because of my parents' failures. I can't put her through that. It..." His jaw tightened. "It messed me up, feeling like an outsider in my own community."

"But your parents weren't living right. They walked away. That's why people rejected them."

"I did the same."

"You were a child. It wasn't your choice."

"I haven't been a child for a long time, Leah. I could have come back. Everyone knows that."

Leah's lip quivered. She looked like she would cry, but

she managed to hold back the tears. "But you're here now. That's all that matters."

"It means a lot to me that you see it that way."

Leah reached out and took his hand. The simple gesture warmed his heart and almost made him feel that what she said was true. She believed in him. Maybe others could too. "I asked you to trust me."

John frowned. "About this too?"

"About everything."

John exhaled, then squeezed her hand. "Okay. I'll trust you. But I don't want you to get hurt when it doesn't work out."

Leah raised up on her tiptoes and put her pointer finger over his lips. "Shhhh. Don't tell me it's not going to work out. It's Christmastime. Miracles happen this time of year." She lowered her finger and dropped back to the soles of her feet.

John smiled. "With everything that's happened, I nearly forgot. Today is Christmas Eve, isn't it?"

"And you're going to spend Christmas here, with us. No matter what happens, we will always have that."

"And leave the day after."

"*Nee*. That's Second Christmas. You know we celebrate that day too." Leah looked up at him with pleading eyes. "And a lot of *Englischers* will still be on vacation too. It won't be a *gut* day to move."

"You said forty-eight hours."

"I'm raising it to seventy-two."

John could not resist the sparkle of hope in her eyes. She wanted him here, with her. She accepted him. How could he say no to that? And anyway, she was right. The day after Christmas was a terrible day to move. A smile appeared on John's face. "Okay, you win."

"Then it's decided. You'll stay through Second Christmas."

"And then—"

"*Nee.* We won't talk about that. We'll have Christmas together and you'll trust me. *Ya?*"

John's smile widened to a grin. Suddenly he was filled with all the expectation and excitement of Christmas that he had felt as a child. He could not imagine missing it. Even more, he wanted to experience it with the woman he loved, even if it would be the only one they ever shared together.

Leah was on a mission. She had a plan and she would not let anything stop her. There was no time for breakfast. Instead, she marched straight from the goat barn to the outbuilding where the buggy was parked, hitched up Clyde and headed down the long gravel driveway, toward the highway.

"You haven't eaten!" Miriam shouted from the front porch as Leah drove away.

"I'll be fine!" Leah shouted back, then slapped the reins. Clyde picked up the pace, jolting Leah against the leather bench seat as the buggy rattled forward. She would have plenty to eat where she was going. Viola Esch would never let anyone leave her house on an empty stomach.

The fields and rolling hills were covered in a clean, crisp coat of new fallen snow. The tree branches lining the road dipped toward the ground, heavy with ice. Leah passed a red barn and silo with roofs frosted white with snow. Smoke rose from the chimney of the farmhouse beside them. A group of boys bundled up in scarves, black coats and black felt hats pulled a sled uphill, their small boots dinting the unbroken snow. Leah waved and they waved back.

Leah turned onto a side road that led to a covered bridge with icicles hanging from the trusses. Clyde's hooves echoed across the wooden boards as he trotted through the enclosed space. Leah tucked her black cloak tighter beneath her chin. The temperature was dropping, just in time for the holidays. They would have a white Christmas tomorrow, for sure. Nothing would melt in this weather.

Leah tugged on the reins when she reached a small beige farmhouse with a covered front porch. A single white candle flickered in each window, and the porch railing was wrapped in evergreen boughs. Clyde whinnied, shook his mane and turned into the driveway. "Whoa," Leah murmured. He pulled on the bit and shook his head again. The buggy rocked, then shuddered to a stop. Leah leaped out, slipped on the snow and grabbed the side of the buggy for balance. Clyde swung his head around and snorted. Leah laughed, patted his neck, then hurried to tie the reins to the hitching post. She felt a surge of adrenaline pushing her forward. This had to work.

By the time Leah knocked on the front door, her stomach was full of butterflies. All she could think about was the look in John's eyes when he told her that he had to leave the Amish. She had seen that he wanted to stay. But she had also seen the rejection. He had to know that he was wanted. And he had to have the money to pay the medical bills. Leah whispered a prayer. This was beyond what she could do on her own. She needed *Gott*'s help.

Snow began to fall softly from the sky. The neighboring farm twinkled with white Christmas lights, and she could hear Christmas carols drifting across the yard from their house. Hope swelled within her. Anything felt possible at Christmastime.

The door creaked open, and Viola motioned her inside.

"Don't stand out there and catch cold," she said as she let the door go and began hobbling toward the kitchen. Leah caught the screen door before it slammed and slipped inside. "I need to talk to you," Leah said as she followed Viola into the kitchen.

"Of course you do." Viola's cane rapped against the linoleum floor as she walked toward the counter. "Why else would you be here?" She reached for a carafe sitting beside a cookie tin and a tattered book open to a gingerbread recipe. "I'll pour the *kaffi.* Start talking."

Ten minutes later, Viola was shooing Leah out the door. "There's no time to waste." She pushed a red-checkered cloth into Leah's hand. "Don't forget your ham biscuit. You can eat on the road."

Leah hesitated. "Do you really think it will work?"

"Of course it will. Now, you get going, and I'll head out in the other direction. Oh, and I'll tell Eliza right away. We need to get her in on this. Meet me back here at lunchtime, and we'll see how far we've gotten."

Leah's stomach was churning and her skin felt hot, despite the chilly weather. "He doesn't think anyone wants him here," Leah blurted out. She wished she could take it back as soon as she spoke. She didn't want to betray John's confidence. But her fears for him had pushed the words out before she could stop them.

"I know that."

"You do?"

"It's clear as day. Just like it's clear that you love him. Now, get going with our plan, and we'll find out if folks want him here or not."

The next few hours would determine the rest of Leah's life and whether she spent it with the man she loved.

Chapter Twelve

The day passed in a blur. Leah made it home in time for the evening milking, her fingers numb from gripping the reins through her thin cotton gloves. She cupped her hands and blew on them as she strode into the goat barn.

"Hey." Benjamin straightened up from where he had been leaning over the milking table. "Where have you been all day? It's Christmas Eve, you know."

"I told John I'd be out most of the day. Did he give you the message?"

"Ya." Benjamin scratched his head. "But he didn't say why."

"Don't ask too many questions around Christmas."

"You sound like *Mamm*," Naomi said as she reached for a milk pail. Their mother had always loved planning Christmas surprises. The Amish only gave simple presents, but they felt as special as anything fancy or expensive when Leah opened them on Christmas morning.

"Remember the year *Daed* made us wooden sleds for Christmas?" Amanda asked. "And Benjamin almost found them hidden in the barn by accident?"

Miriam chuckled. "*Ya. Mamm* had to work hard to distract you so I could move them behind a bale of hay."

"You were in on that?" Naomi asked.

"Ya," Miriam said. "And we surprised you, ain't so?"

Naomi smiled. *"Ya."*

"That was a *wunderbar* Christmas," Benjamin said. "There was lots of snow, remember?"

Amanda smiled. "We spent the whole day sledding."

The room fell silent as they all remembered. No one said that it had been their last Christmas with their parents, but Leah knew they were all thinking it. Enough time had passed that she could feel warm and happy inside at the memory, despite the loss. They had had good times together. And now, if her plan worked, there would be many happy Christmases to come.

"So, you've been out Christmas shopping for us, huh?" Benjamin raised his eyebrows.

"Um, not exactly." Leah wondered how to explain what she was doing. It was better to keep it to herself in case she failed. "Didn't I just tell you not to ask too many questions this close to Christmas?"

Benjamin laughed. "Okay. Got it. Just remember I need a new scarf."

Leah rolled her eyes.

Miriam unlatched a goat from a milking table and patted her on the rump. "Go on now," she said. The goat scurried to the ground. Miriam turned to Leah before bringing the next goat onto the table. "John didn't leave today. So he must be staying for Christmas."

"*Ya*. I convinced him to stay. No one moves over the holidays."

"But he *is* moving." Miriam studied Leah's reaction. "Right?"

Leah looked down. "*Ach*, I don't know."

"Leah, he wants to go back to the *Englisch*. You have

to let him go." Miriam leaned her hip against the milking table as she waited for Leah's response.

"*Vell*, what if he did stay?" Leah asked.

Miriam sighed. "He's got that *Englisch* job, ain't so? I thought his heart was already set on it."

"But if he wanted to stay?" Leah narrowed her eyes. "Would you support that?"

"If he's willing to live as Amish. He'd have to be baptized to stay here long-term."

"Right. So if he took the kneeling vows, you'd welcome him?"

Miriam frowned. "Where is this going, Leah?"

"I don't know. Just answer my question."

"I would," Benjamin said. "For certain sure."

"*Danki*, Benji." Leah looked over to him with a smile. "I knew you would."

Benjamin returned the smile before turning his attention back to the milking machine.

Miriam exchanged a concerned glance with Amanda and Naomi.

Amanda stood up from her milking stool. "We don't want you to get hurt."

"But what if he wanted to get baptized?" Leah asked. "Would you hold his past against him?"

"As long as he supports you, we would support him," Naomi said.

"Wait. What does this have to do with me?" Leah tried to look offended.

"Nice try," Miriam said. "We all know that this has everything to do with you." Miriam closed her eyes, rubbed her temples, then lowered her hand. "You always said you'd never settle down with a man, especially an *Englischer*. Are you sure about this?"

"Hey! I never said I was looking to settle down with John."

"You didn't have to," Miriam said.

"Is it really that obvious?"

"Ya!" All three siblings shouted at once.

"Oh. Okay." Leah looked away.

"Don't be embarrassed," Miriam said. "We all fall for someone eventually, whether we want to or not."

"You haven't," Leah muttered under her breath.

"I heard that," Miriam said. "And leave me out of this."

"You said *we*."

"Figure of speech."

"Fine." Leah shot Miriam a look. "So will you accept him?"

Miriam hesitated. "How do you feel when you're around him?"

"Like someone sees me for the first time."

Miriam didn't say anything for a moment. Then she nodded. "That's what matters, Leah. If he commits to the faith and that's truly the way he makes you feel, then *ya*, I'll accept him. *Nee*, more than that. I'll welcome him. I made the mistake of holding Emma's past against her before she married Benji, and I won't do that again." Her expression shifted. "But Leah, are you sure he wants to stay? And even if he does, it may not be possible."

"If he does, I have to do everything I can to make it possible."

"So that's what you've been up to all day," Benjamin said.

"Don't tell John." Leah glanced behind her.

Amanda laughed. "He's not standing behind you, Leah."

Leah gave a sheepish smile. "*Vell*, you never know.

And I'm not taking any chances. I don't want to get his hopes up."

Miriam put her hands on her hips. "Leah, what exactly are you going to do?"

"I'm not *going* to do anything." Leah gave a sly smile. "I've already done it. Now we wait to see what will happen."

John had forgotten the magic of Christmas Eve. For years, the day before Christmas had felt like any other day, except for the advertisements trying to convince him to buy expensive gifts for family he did not have. He used to pick up a carton of eggnog from the grocery store on his way home from work, then collapse onto the couch and watch old Christmas movies. Sometimes he could hear people nearby, gathering to celebrate together. He used to turn up his television to drown out the loneliness.

But this Christmas Eve he was surrounded by people who were smiling and laughing with expectation of the coming holiday. The Stoltzfus family still had to work, of course, but there was plenty of cheer to go around while they fed and milked the goats, chopped wood or did the Christmas baking. After lunch, Miriam had served fruitcake and eggnog before they headed back to work. This was real, homemade eggnog, sprinkled with nutmeg. John had forgotten how rich and creamy it could be.

The only problem that day—except for his constant worry over Abby—had been that Leah was not there. She had taken off before breakfast and did not return until it was time for the evening milking. He wondered what she was up to and why she thought she could solve an impossible problem. She had said to trust her, and he wanted to. But he had been through enough to have become a realist. He did not expect a miracle, even at Christmas. So, he would make the most of the short, precious time that he had left at Stoneybrook Farm.

When Leah came in from the goat barn, she met him with a warm smile before immediately checking on Abby.

"How is she?" Leah moved the blanket aside so she could get a better look at Abby's face as she slept in John's arms.

"She's doing well, for now," John said. He slid his eyes from Abby to Leah. "What about you? You got any news for me?"

"*Ach, nee.* Except that Christmas Eve dinner is almost ready."

John did not push her. He was going to try his best to live in the moment.

After a dinner of ham, sweet potato casserole, cranberry sauce and homemade sourdough bread, the family sang Christmas carols by candlelight. The fire inside the woodstove flickered orange behind the grate and warmed the room. But John's heart was already warm. In that moment of song, with the dim light flickering across the holly garlands and highlighting the sparkle in Leah's eyes, John felt like he had finally come home. Abby woke up and stirred in his arms. He wished he could give her this moment, this family forever.

Except he still wasn't sure that the entire family wanted him here.

John stole a glance at Miriam and caught her watching him. She looked away quickly, but John could sense the judgment in her eyes. Or was it just concern? He could not tell and he did not want to ask. Not now, on Christmas Eve. It would be too hard to bear if she told him something he did not want to hear.

Christmas dawned clear and bright, with sunlight sparkling off a fresh coat of soft white snow. The woodstove filled the farmhouse with heat, making the rooms feel cozy and snug. The scent of wood smoke mingled with the smell of fresh-cut pine decorating the windowsills and dining room table. This was a day that the Amish traditionally spent fasting and praying in somber reflection. That came naturally to John at a time like this. He had a lot to pray for this year, and it felt good to give all his cares to *Gott*, even though his stomach complained.

When they broke their fast at dinner, the mood shifted to lively banter. John caught himself smiling and laughing, despite the heavy burden weighing him down. Amanda kept refilling his glass of eggnog, and Naomi pushed an extra slice of pumpkin pie onto his plate. He wondered if they were being more welcoming because his baby was sick. That would make sense. Or could they be trying to reach out and bridge the gap between them? Should he say something? No, he didn't want to disrupt such a pleasant dinner. And besides, he would be leaving soon. No sense in stirring up trouble when they would not see each other again after this.

"Who wants to go sledding?" Benjamin asked after he polished off a second slice of fruitcake.

"Not me," Miriam said. "There's too much to do to prepare for Second Christmas. I'm sure we'll have lots of visitors. But you should go on. I'll watch the *bopplin*."

"I want to!" Leah jumped up from the table. "Let's go, John."

"I should stay with Abby." John looked down at his baby sleeping peacefully in a bassinet beside the table, where he could keep an eye on her while they ate.

"I'll take care of her," Miriam said. "She's fast asleep and won't even know you're gone. Besides, you'll be right outside the house. I'll let you know if she needs you." Miriam paused and looked at him carefully before adding, "You could use the break, John."

"Come on." Leah tugged on his arm until he smiled, shook his head and stood up.

"Okay, okay, you win." He couldn't hide his excitement at being included.

They spent the next hour careening down the hill together. Darkness spread across the hillside, but the white snow reflected the moonlight, making the night unnaturally bright. Leah's cheeks turned red with cold, but she never stopped smiling, even after her cloak became damp from the snow. John felt like a child again. He could not remember the last time he had had this much fun. Benjamin kept racing them up and down the hill, until they collapsed from exhaustion and headed back inside to warm up with mugs of hot chocolate by the woodstove.

Soon, it was time for bed and Christmas Day was at an end. But the peaceful warmth stayed with John long after he put Abby to bed, as he lay awake beneath the quilt, listening to the howl of the wind. *Help me to accept that I have to leave, Gott,* he whispered into the quiet darkness. *Or if it is Your will, make a way for me to stay. Please. Amen.* He turned over and listened to the sound of Abby's soft, even breath. *But only if I am wanted here,* he added. *Only if the community will accept my daughter. Amen again and good night.* John wasn't sure that it was okay to say good night after a prayer. It felt a little too informal. But he liked the idea of God being a friend that he could talk to like that. He fell asleep remembering the gleam in Leah's eyes as they raced down the hill together and wondering what tomorrow would bring. She had said to trust her. He hoped with all his heart that he could.

* * *

The next morning, John woke up to the sound of horse hooves clattering up the driveway. Buggy wheels crunched in the snow. A shout rang out, followed by Leah's voice. He could not make out the words. He threw off the quilt and sat up quickly. Had he overslept? He pulled open the green shade. No, the sun was still beneath the horizon, the sky above the tree line glowing faintly in the darkness. Second Christmas was the day the Amish celebrated by visiting each other and exchanging simple gifts, but it seemed too early for that to start yet.

John threw on his black broadfall trousers and his best-for-Sunday shirt. Abby stirred and woke as he dressed. "Happy Second Christmas," he said as he scooped her up and hurried out of the room. His heart pounded as he strode down the hallway. He felt alert and alive. Was everything okay? Was there more bad news coming their way? Or could it be something good? A horse whinnied outside, followed by the jangle of metal. Someone was parking in the yard. John walked to the door and flung it open, letting a cold blast of winter air into the house.

He stared into the farmyard, unsure what to make of what he was seeing. It wasn't just one buggy out front. Three buggies were pulling in, and a fourth one was heading up the driveway. A fifth buggy turned off the highway as he watched. "What's going on?" he wondered aloud.

Footsteps pounded down the hallway behind him. He turned to see Leah racing toward him, grinning. "I saw them out the kitchen window! They came, John!"

"What do you mean? What's going on?"

Leah stepped around him and pushed the door open all the way. She motioned to the crowd gathering in the yard. "*Kumme* in!" she shouted. "*Kumme* in!"

There were several familiar faces tying horses to hitching posts or scrambling out of buggies. Amos and Edna, Viola, Gabriel and Eliza, as well as people he did not recognize. "Why are they all here?" John asked Leah.

Amos overheard as he trotted up the porch steps with a sly twinkle in his eye. "We're here for you! Merry Christmas, John. We have a present for you."

John frowned as he processed the information. He wasn't sure how to react. "For me?" he asked slowly.

Amos chuckled, winked at Leah and slapped John on the back. "For certain sure. Now, how about some *kaffi* cake? Edna made it last night." Edna waved from the farmyard and held up a tin decorated with snowmen and Christmas trees.

Five minutes later, the living room was packed with excited families sipping strong black coffee and nibbling on coffee cake. A few children had slipped outside, and their shouts drifted into the house as they played in the snow. "Now that we're all here, it's time we told John what's going on," Amos said.

A round of laughter passed through the room.

Viola pointed her cane at Leah. "You tell him, Leah. This was all your idea."

Amos nodded at her.

An expectant hush fell across the room. John's heart beat hard in his chest. He dared to hope that his prayers were about to be answered.

"Oll recht," Leah said. She squeezed John's arm. "The entire district has come together to pay for Abby's medical expenses. We raised the money for the surgery in just two days."

John stared at her. He could not believe what he was hearing. He swallowed hard.

"How?" The entire district had rallied behind him? Was that really possible?

"Simple. I told Viola, and she told Eliza, and they helped me set everything in motion. You know how fast word travels on the Amish telegraph. On Christmas Eve, we went from house to house, explaining the situation. Then people from those houses went out and spread the word, and *vell*, pretty soon the whole county was involved. Then folks called family and friends in Ohio and Indiana. Amos gave us permission to use the phone because it's a medical emergency. And those people in Ohio and Indiana went out and spread the word. So now, you've got donations from Amish folks from all over America. I think we even got some from Canada."

"We did," Viola piped up. "From the Aylmer, Ontario Amish."

"But..." John shook his head. Abby shifted in his arms, and suddenly John understood. She was a precious, innocent baby who deserved their help. Who could say no to that? "What an amazing thing to do for my baby." He swallowed down the lump forming in his throat. "I don't know how to thank you enough."

Amos walked across the room, put an arm on John's shoulder and looked him squarely in the eye. "It wasn't just for Abby. It was for you, John. We want you to stay here, where you belong."

When Amos stepped back, Leah slipped closer and took John's hand. It was a bold move in front of a room full of people, but no one seemed to mind. They were all too caught up in the moment. It was the greatest Christmas present any of them had ever witnessed, and they were all a part of it.

"Amish from all over North America are welcoming you back, John," Bishop Amos said.

John felt such a flood of emotion that his knees were weak. He was on the verge of tears and laughter at the same time. The joy of Christmas flooded his heart while he stared at the crowd gathered here, just for him, welcoming him home as the fire crackled in the woodstove and the candles in the windowsills flickered within wreaths of holly. They wanted him here. All of them. Sure, there were probably a few people who would still judge him, but that was okay. Enough people had proven that he was one of them, despite the fact that he had refused to believe it.

Nothing would keep him away now.

"I want to take the kneeling vows," he blurted out.

Leah threw her arms around him and Abby, in the warmest, truest hug he'd ever experienced. A shout rang out across the room, followed by applause. "I've been so afraid," Leah whispered in his ear. "But I'm not afraid anymore."

He could barely make out her words above the noise of the crowd. But he could feel them, all the way down to his bones. "You never have to be afraid again," he whispered back. "I'm here to stay, for good. We're going to be a family."

"I love you," Leah murmured in his ear.

"I love you too," John whispered. Even though they were in a room full of people, for that perfect moment, it felt as if they were the only ones in the entire universe. There was just him, the woman he loved and the baby in his arms that they would raise together.

Then John remembered the only problem left. He looked over Leah's head to Miriam. "Am I still welcome here, in your home?" he asked.

"For certain sure," Miriam said. "You're one of us now, ain't so?"

And John knew in his heart that it was true.

"Maybe there's something else you want to say?" Amos leaned over and whispered to John.

John crinkled his brow. He had already thanked them. But he probably should thank them again. This was the best Christmas present anyone could ever give or get. Not only was his daughter taken care of, but they had both received the gift of belonging. *"Danki,"* he said, automatically slipping in the old, familiar Pennsylvania Dutch.

"You're welcome. But I was thinking what you had to say might be in the form of a question." He raised his eyebrows.

John took a few beats, then it hit him what the bishop meant. Leah looked up at him with nervous, hopeful eyes. The idea made him feel dizzy with happiness. But right here, in front of everyone? He leaned down and whispered in Leah's ear. "Now? With them all watching? And after we've only known each other for such a short amount of time?"

She nodded. "We can have a long engagement, to make sure. But it would make me feel safe to know that you're all in. I think I need that."

"I am." He grinned at her, then felt suddenly sheepish. The room fell silent. Everyone stared at him. He cleared his throat. "Can you hold Abby for a moment?" he asked Amos.

"Of course," he said as John handed her over. She was sleeping peacefully through all the noise and excitement.

John glanced around the room, then at Leah. He knew what the answer would be, but he still felt nervous. He dropped to one knee and took her hand. "I don't know if the Amish kneel to ask this question, but it feels like the right thing to do. Sorry if I've got it wrong."

"You've got everything right, John," Leah murmured, her eyes staring deeply into his.

"Will you marry me?"

"Ya!" Leah nearly shouted the word. "I certain sure will!"

The room exploded with cheers.

It was the happiest Christmas of John's life, the one when a miracle took place, even though he did not think it was possible. But now he knew, dreams really do come true at Christmastime, that magical time of year when anything can happen.

Epilogue

The next few months of medical procedures and hospital stays for Abby weren't easy to go through, but John was surrounded by a community that loved and supported him. That made him feel like he could get through almost anything. The surgery was successful, and the doctors were optimistic that Abby wouldn't need any more, although they would have to monitor her closely for a long time to come. The donations kept pouring in, so John knew that he did not have to worry about paying for whatever care she might need in the years ahead.

He and Leah took their engagement slowly. It felt good to give themselves the time to learn to trust again, without pressure. Sometimes, as she waited for wedding season that fall, Leah's old fears would rush back and she would have to catch her breath and remind herself that John was his own man, with his own choices. He was not Steve. And he proved his commitment to her every day, until she finally believed it, deep in her heart. On the morning of their wedding day, she woke up and realized that she did not doubt him, not even in the darkest corners of her mind where her worst fears once hid. She was not afraid anymore. She finally trusted him, fully and completely.

So, when Bishop Amos asked her to say the words that

would tie them together for the rest of their lives, Leah had no reservations. As she stood in front of the congregation wearing a blue cape dress sewn especially for her wedding, she knew that this marriage was the right thing to do. And all of the pain, all of the waiting, was worth it now. Because she had found the man who valued her for who she was, no matter what. And she felt the same way about him.

There were quite a few comments during the reception, especially from Viola. "I knew you hadn't really sworn off men," she said as she thumped her cane against the floor to emphasize her words.

"Just not this man," Leah quipped.

John laughed and squeezed her hand.

They moved into the new addition that John had started building before either of them dreamed that this would be their future. The room was just big enough for a queen bed, a crib and Leah's hope chest. It felt cozy and snug, perfect for the three of them. John loved sharing the rest of the house with the big, boisterous Stoltzfus family. *His* family now.

Abby was crawling now and would be walking soon. The months were flying past, and they treasured each moment together. The days were busy with farmwork, and they worked side by side, when John wasn't taking care of odd jobs or construction projects around the property. The evenings were filled with big family dinners and lots of laughter, like John had always wanted.

He and Leah both had the family they had always dreamed of, but never dared to believe they could have. Most evenings after dinner they would sit on the enclosed back porch and watch the sun go down as they held hands. Leah liked to lean her head against John's shoulder. They would talk about things that mattered to her, and she felt seen and heard in a way she had never believed possible. He would revel in the quiet sanctuary they had created, where life was simple and good and he knew he was accepted.

"I love you, John," Leah murmured as they watched the sky fade into soft shades of purple. A bird darted across the sky as the wind whispered through the oak leaves. "And I love you, Leah." He wrapped an arm around her and pulled her closer. "I will never let you go."

And she knew it was true.

* * * * *

Dear Reader,

I am so excited to welcome you to Stoneybrook Farm. I hope you enjoyed the first book in my new miniseries. John's journey to find a place to belong was long and arduous, but he finally found his way home—and just in time for Christmas. My hope for all of us, especially during this season of miracles, is that we are blessed with a sense of belonging, no matter where we call home.

Look for the next book in the Sisters of Stoneybrook Farm miniseries to learn which sister will find love next. And, in the meantime, you can visit the quaint little village of Bluebird Hills, where their farm is located, in my previous books. Have a very merry Christmas and a happy New Year.

Love always,
Virginia Wise